BORROWED TROUBLE

BORROWED TROUBLE

A Melanie Bass Mystery

CHRISTINE FALCONE

First published by Level Best Books 2023

Author Photo Credit: Sara McIngvale Photography

First edition

ISBN: 978-1-68512-461-8

Cover art by Level Best Designs

This book was professionally typeset on Reedsy.
Find out more at reedsy.com

For My Family with Much Love

Chapter One

"I need to borrow your dog."

It took a moment for me to recognize the woman standing at my door. It had been over two months since Detective Sunny Cody had been involved in solving the murder of my ex-husband. She was dressed in jeans and a crew neck sweater, much more casually than I had ever seen her.

I stood there in stunned silence for a few moments. "What do you mean, you need to borrow Bruno? Why?" What was she doing here and with such a bizarre request? My little terrier mix, Bruno, had come with me to answer the doorbell. His short tail was wagging eagerly as I opened the front door. Now he backed up to stand behind me, his nose pushed into the back of my legs.

"May I come in and explain?" Detective Cody looked over her shoulder, as if she expected to see someone behind her.

I stepped aside and waved her in. I motioned for her to take a seat on the sofa but instead, she remained standing. "I am working on a case now that involves some individuals that we think are distributing illegal substances in this neighborhood." She hesitated for a moment, then continued. "I need a way to observe them, and if possible, to witness some of their illegal activity."

It was unsettling to think of drugs being sold in this quiet corner of town, though of course, I knew it happened all over. But why come to me? "How does this have anything to do with Bruno? Don't you usually just set up a stake out or whatever it's called somewhere you can observe the people you're after?"

She looked away and sighed, then back at me. "Unfortunately, that didn't work. The supplier spotted our car right away and no exchange of money or product was made. Our informant tells us they have moved the meeting spot to a more secluded, and they assume less accessible, spot. A parked car they didn't expect would be obvious. A person walking, especially walking a dog, wouldn't stand out. So, I ask again, may I borrow your dog?"

I looked down at Bruno. The little terrier was now looking nervously at Detective Cody and then up at me. Both Bruno and I had been put in danger after Artie's murder, and both of us were still dealing with the aftermath. I shook my head. "No. I'm sorry Detective, I'd like to help you, but my dog has been through enough in the past couple of months. I don't want him involved in anything that might prove stressful to him again."

"But I know you walk your dog. How will this be stressful for him? I assure you he won't be in any danger. I just need a plausible reason to be on that back road when we were told a sale and exchange would be made. There are other officers set to move in to make the arrest when I notify them that it has occurred." She looked expectantly at me, "So?"

"Why don't you use a police dog? Aren't they trained to respond in instances like that?"

"For the very reason you just named. Our police canines are well-trained in how to react when in the presence of a perpetrator. They are also large and could appear intimidating. I want a little frou-frou-looking dog that won't raise anyone's suspicions. Besides, I assume people, including the criminals involved, are used to seeing your dog being walked around the neighborhood."

I felt my own hackles rise at her description of Bruno. "Look, my dog may be small, but he is not 'frou-frou' by any means. He acted very bravely in the face of danger not very long ago...."

"I apologize. I meant no insult. I just meant I want a civilian-looking dog."

I didn't answer her right away. It was true that the drug problem in town had become more severe. I had several patients recently who had been either the victim of a drug-related crime or had injured themselves while under the influence of illegal drugs and required the services of the home health care agency that I worked for.

Detective Cody cleared her throat. "We would really like to get the guy behind this. He could be a valuable link to the larger operation." She pulled her cell phone from her jeans pocket and looked at it. "I have to know now; our sources say the deal will be going down shortly."

I looked at Bruno. No way I was going to let him go this alone. "I'm coming with you."

"No. Absolutely not. This is a police operation. I can't take a civilian with me."

"You said Bruno would be in no danger, so it should be safe for me to go along also. If I don't go, he doesn't go." I gave her my best stare-down.

Detective Cody's phone pinged, and she glanced down at it and sighed. "I forgot you were sort of a pain in the neck." She looked as if she was making up her mind about something, then said," Okay, but we have to get moving now."

I took Bruno's leash from the peg by the door and hooked it to his collar. As we headed out the door, Detective Cody reached for the leash. "I don't want this to look suspicious, so I think I better take the dog's leash. We could chat as we get closer, as if I'm a trainer you hired or your new dog walker." She gave me a tight smile.

We headed toward the area where Detective Cody said the drug deal was to occur. Bruno walked jauntily along, looking over at me every few steps as if to make sure I was still there. However, Detective Cody held the leash as if it was a poisonous snake – arm extended out stiffly and leash stretched up taut.

"Detective, no one is going to believe you are either a trainer or have even ever walked a dog in your life." I reached for the leash, "May I?" I took Bruno's leash and showed her how to hold it. I then gave Bruno the soft command to "heel," and he snapped to my left heel. "Did you ever have a dog growing up?" I asked her.

"My sister had allergies. We had fish."

I handed Bruno's leash back to her. We had just reached the end of my road, about to turn toward the unpaved road that ran between an area of brush and trees on one side and the tidal marsh on the other, when she stopped and looked at me. "As I said, I don't expect a problem, but if I tell you to stop, or to get back, you take the dog, and you do just that. No discussion, no argument. Understand?"

I had forgotten she could be such a hard ass. Not that I would have argued with her anyway. I had no desire to be involved in any more police activity after my last experience when Artie was murdered. "Understood."

She handed Bruno's leash back to me, and she took out her phone again and appeared to be texting someone.

"Don't you have a police radio or something? I mean in case you need somebody in a hurry?"

She reached behind to the waistband of her jeans at the small of her back. "Yes, but they may not be the only ones listening. I have it in case of emergency, and for when we've witnessed the drug exchange. For now, I've sent the message we are about to approach the subjects and will radio when appropriate and tell them to move in." She took back Bruno's leash and said, "Ready? Let's see if our information is correct."

It was the beginning of October and one of my favorite times of year in Connecticut. Today was warm enough that a jacket wasn't necessary, and I only had on a long sleeve sweater and jeans, dressed very similarly to Detective Cody. I had to admit we did look like just two suburban women out for a stroll with a dog. At least, I hoped so. We didn't talk for a few moments, but walked side by side, Bruno walking very nicely to Detective Cody's left. I loved this part of my walks with Bruno; the dirt road snaked for a mile in a loop. On the left, woods stretched for a mile and a half, part of a land preserve and hiking trail, so there were no houses. On the right was marshland rich with birds and small wildlife. Despite our mission, I couldn't help but start to relax.

Suddenly, a question popped into my mind. "I'm surprised you're investigating this drug ring," I said. "I thought you only dealt with murder investigations."

She didn't look at me, but I could see her mouth tense for a moment. "I wasn't aware you were an expert on the workings of the police department. I appreciate your help in this situation, but you don't need to worry about the how and why of it."

I was about to tell her that I meant no offense, but as we rounded a slight curve in the road, I noticed a Saab SUV with tinted windows pulled to the right side of the road about one hundred yards ahead of us. There was someone standing beside the passenger side door using binoculars to peer across the marshland. It looked like a man, but it was hard to tell, as whoever it was had long hair flowing from beneath a ball cap pulled low on their forehead. Detective Cody seemed to tense slightly, and one hand went toward the small of her back. As if by agreement, I took Bruno's leash from her other hand.

"You don't think they are just bird watching, do you?" I said.

She shook her head, "No. That's the description of the vehicle we received the tip about. Let's just keep walking, slowly as if we're in no hurry. When we get abreast of them, do you think you can get the dog to poop, so you can pause to pick it up? I want to see if I can see who is in the car."

I gave her a disgusted look. "Bruno is good, but I haven't yet taught him to poop on command. I can stop and pretend I have a pebble in my shoe or something."

"All right, that will do."

As we approached the Saab, the man scanning the marshes turned briefly to glance at us. As he took the binoculars away for a moment, I thought he looked directly at Detective Cody, then pulled the bill of his cap further over his forehead. I waved "hello" but he quickly turned away and pulled up the collar of the light jacket he was wearing to further obscure his face.

"What are you doing!" Detective Cody said in a harsh whisper.

"Just trying to look like a friendly neighbor."

As it happened, Bruno did oblige and began sniffing in circles as we were abreast of the vehicle. As I bent, poop bag in hand, ready to clean up after him, two things happened. First, there was a bellow of "Shiloh!" coming from the opposite direction, followed by the woman who lived down the road from me. She was chasing her galloping Husky as he dragged a leash behind. This was followed by a cloud of dust as a car came too quickly around the bend behind her. I screamed, "watch out!" to her as the speeding car approached. Shiloh veered into the woods, and the woman, Bruno, and I dove after him to avoid being run over by the car. I heard several pops, then a thump. The speeding car raced away, quickly followed by the Saab, which sped off in the opposite direction. I dusted myself off as I got up from the clump of brush I had jumped into. I grabbed Bruno's leash again and looked around for Detective Cody. She was lying in the dirt road, several paces back from the rest of us, struggling to get up.

Her face was covered in dirt, and she was trying to move her right leg, but I could see by its unnatural angle that wasn't a good idea. "Detective! Hold still, I'll get help!" I could hear sobbing behind me. It was my neighbor.

"What just happened? Why was that maniac speeding like that? We were almost killed!" I turned to see that Shiloh had had the good grace to return to his owner and was licking her face as she clung to his neck.

I rushed to Detective Cody. "Did that car hit you? Don't move until we get help."

She grunted. "Just clipped me. Only my leg." She was still struggling to get up. And in spite of what she said, I could tell she was having trouble breathing, and she had blood dripping from a wound on her forehead at her hairline.

I helped her into a semi-sitting position. Her face was white, and she groaned with any slight movement. "The radio—hand it to me." Her voice came out in short gasps.

I saw the police radio that had been tucked into the back of her waistband, now lying several feet away in the dirt. "It looks like it was run over by one of the cars."

"Then help me get my phone out of my back pocket. I need to call the team. Let them know what happened," she said.

I pulled out my own phone. "First, I'm calling 911. You need medical attention right away." I made the call, then carefully worked the cell phone from her pocket, trying not to make her move more than necessary.

Detective Cody leaned on one elbow as she made the call to the backup team. She told them that the Saab was where they were told it would be and that the second car had appeared and began shooting at the Saab before both had screeched away. "No, I didn't." She looked up at me, "Did anyone see what make of car the second one was?"

My neighbor had stopped sobbing and was just sniffling now. "White or cream colored. Right before Shiloh pulled away, I heard it coming down the road and turned to see who was going so fast on this road. I think it was maybe an Accord or something like that."

I nodded. "Definitely mid-sized. And I think she's right, it was light colored."

I noticed Detective Cody didn't mention to whoever she was speaking to that she had been hurt in the exchange between the cars.

The detective looked at me. "The guy with binoculars? Did he make it back into the car before the Saab took off?"

I looked around. I had forgotten momentarily about the man standing outside the first car. I walked over to where he had been. There was blood on the sea grass on the slope leading down to the marsh, and half submerged in the water was a blood-stained, crumpled form. I looked back toward Cody and shook my head.

The sound of the responding emergency vehicles and police cars was deafening. I had looped Bruno's leash over a branch while I tended to Detective Cody, but now ran over to scoop him up before he hurt himself while struggling to run away from the sound. Shiloh just sat and howled along with the approaching sirens.

I squatted down next to Detective Cody as the EMTs unloaded their stretcher and several police officers jumped from their vehicles. One of the officers strode over to where she was lying. "It seems you left out an important bit of information, Detective." He motioned toward her bleeding head and bent leg.

She grunted and said, "I'm not in the mood Langley." She waved him away.

"How bad is it?" He continued to stand over her.

"I'll live. I think." She was pale, and her jaw was set tightly.

I looked up at the officer. "Let's let the EMTs see to her; you can talk to her when she's more comfortable."

He gave me a long look as if assessing my right to give him any kind of instructions, then he nodded and walked away to join the two officers on the slope to the marsh.

I turned back to Detective Cody. "It's okay to scream or swear a little bit if it will help. There isn't much I haven't heard, you know." I had a feeling Detective Cody never said much beyond an occasional "damn," but I hoped a little levity would help. I had converted to the numb action mode I used in medical emergencies. I'd process what happened later.

She gave me a grimace meant to be a smile, but said, "I'm sorry."

"About what?"

"Dog. I said wouldn't be in danger. You too. Sorry."

I just laid a hand on her shoulder. "Let's just get you to the hospital. Bruno is all right, and so am I." I didn't add that it was my fault, too, for not listening to my own intuition about not letting Bruno and myself get involved in a police case again.

As the EMTs loaded the detective onto the stretcher, Officer Langley, the policeman who had been speaking to Detective Cody, came to get my statement.

"I'll need your name and contact information, miss." I could see that another officer was talking to my neighbor, whose name I could not remember for the life of me.

"Melanie Bass, 852 Starbridge Lane." As I recited my phone numbers for him, I watched as a team set up crime scene tape around the area leading down to the marsh to where the man's body was lying.

"So, how did you happen to be in the area when this incident occurred?"

I hesitated briefly, unsure what the protocol was for civilians along on a drug bust. "I was walking with Detective Cody when we came upon the Saab parked by the side of the road." His eyebrows rose slightly, so I added, "It was my fault I was here. Detective Cody refused to let me come along, but I insisted." I didn't know how much my explanation would help, but I'd tried anyway.

"What about the other woman? Was she walking with you?" The officer tipped his head toward my neighbor.

"No." Was her name Amy? "She lives in my neighborhood, and she was walking her dog also. They were coming from the opposite direction," I said.

"Why don't you explain everything that happened exactly as you remember it, starting with when you turned down this road."

I took him through the whole incident: seeing the Saab, the man standing next to it, Shiloh escaping his owner, and the sudden appearance of the second car and the apparent gunshots. "Detective Cody was trying to see into the first car to see if she could see who was in there. I don't know if she got a chance to see anything before the second car came roaring past and hit her."

"What about the man who was shot? Did he say anything to either you or Detective Cody?"

"No."

"Did he seem to be trying to hide or discard anything before he was shot?"

I shook my head, "I really didn't see anything after the second car approached. I was too busy getting both my dog and myself out of the way."

The officer thanked me and went to speak to the other officers at the scene. It looked like they were finished interviewing my neighbor, also. She had gone over to lean against a tree trunk, turned away from the area where the man who had been shot went down the slope. Shiloh was lying with his head resting on her feet. I went over to see if she was going to be all right. My own nerves were starting to be jangled as the reality of what had just happened began to sink in.

"Hello. I'm Melanie Bass. I know you live just a few houses down from me, but I'm afraid I've forgotten your name."

She turned to answer me, a bewildered look on her face. "Audrey Cullen." She shook her head, "I don't get what just happened. That woman who got hurt; she was a cop?" She tipped her head toward the action going on near the marsh. "Is that guy dead?"

I nodded. Bruno and Shiloh had begun sniffing each other, both of them with their tails wagging.

"The other police officer said something about drugs. Do you know what was going on?" she asked.

"I know that Detective Cody thought that there was going to be a drug deal going down here. The police were poised to arrest the dealers, but I don't think anybody expected there to be gunshots fired."

"Drugs? Here?"

I nodded. "I know. It's scary. I guess they figured no one would be around to see them here."

"Are you a cop too? Why were you with her?"

"No, I'm not a cop. I—um—know Detective Cody from earlier this summer. She stopped in to ask a favor of me." I left it at that.

Audrey shifted away from the tree. "Do you think it's okay if we leave now? My son will be coming home from school soon, and I need to drive him to soccer practice."

"I believe so. I think the officers will contact us if they have any more questions."

Detective Cody had long since left in the ambulance, and all the other officers were involved in processing the crime scene. I watched as Audrey and Shiloh left in the direction they had come from earlier, then took one more look around at what had once been my "quiet place." Bruno and I headed for home.

Chapter Two

Once Bruno and I got home, all the feelings I had tucked away during the shooting and the aftermath hit me hard. I sat on the sofa and began to shake. Tears welled up in my eyes, and I felt Bruno nuzzle my knees. I pulled him into my lap and stroked him, trying to calm myself down. I realized how much I missed my former housemate, Lynn Duncan. I wanted to talk to someone about what had just happened; vent my feelings over being in the middle of another violent act so soon after Artie had been killed. I also hoped to get some reassurance that I wasn't crazy for letting Detective Cody talk me into using Bruno in her sting operation.

I was sure Lynn would understand how I felt. We met during the summer after Artie was murdered. Unbeknownst to me at the time, she had been married to him prior to him marrying me. As more and more information came to the surface about Artie and his activities before he was killed, we had become friends as we dealt with the aftermath of his crimes. I had invited her to stay with me since she was from out of town. After deciding to stay in the area permanently, she had just moved out the previous week into a condo one town over. I decided to call her and tell her about what had happened with Detective Cody.

"You'll never guess who showed up at my door this afternoon to ask for help with a police investigation."

"Detective Cody? She asked you for help? Are you kidding, what kind of help could she want?"

"She wanted to use Bruno as a sort of decoy in a set up to arrest some drug dealers who have been operating in town. I only agreed to let her take Bruno if she would take me also." I felt a bit shaky again as I thought about what had happened. "Unfortunately, things did not go well." I recapped for Lynn the afternoon's events. By the time I finished, I had tears leaking down my cheeks as I realized things could have been even worse than they were. I grabbed a tissue off the coffee table. "So, a not so quiet Sunday afternoon after all." I tried to make my voice lighter.

"Are you sure you and Bruno are all right? I mean you didn't get hurt from the speeding car or anything?" She sounded as stunned as I felt when it happened.

"Yes. I don't know about Cody though. She was hurt pretty badly, although she was conscious and speaking when I last saw her. I am giving them some time to examine her and work her up then I'll call the hospital and at least get an update on her condition."

"Good lord Melanie, I can't believe something like this happened to you again. Promise you will lie low, just stay home and read or something. No more involvement in dangerous situations, okay?"

That made me chuckle. "As I recall, the last time I was in a dangerous situation, you were in it right beside me."

"Okay, that is true, but that doesn't mean it was smart. If you get any info on how Detective Cody is, would you let me know? She may have given us a hard time when she was investigating Artie's death, but I kind of liked her. I have a painting class to teach later this afternoon, but you can leave a message, and I'll call you back later."

I waited another hour after I ended my call to Lynn, then I called Patient Information at University Hospital. Before my position as a nurse at Coretrack Homecare, I worked for several years on a medical/surgical floor in the hospital. I kept in contact with some of the staff both in the ED and on my former floor. However, I knew I couldn't pump them for specific information on Detective Cody due to HIPPA. According to Patient Information, she was admitted to an orthopedic floor and was in stable condition. I decided I would call the floor anyway, just get a general idea of what her injuries were. I didn't recognize the name of the unit secretary who answered my call, but when I was connected to her nurse, I lucked out. It was Jacki Avon, a great nurse but one who was prone to oversharing information.

After a few minutes of catching up on what was going on in our lives, I said, "A friend of mine was injured today, a police officer, Sunny Cody. I was wondering if you know how she is doing. When I last saw her, it looked like she had fractured her leg and she was in a lot of pain."

"Holy Moly, don't tell me you were there!"

"Yes, we were walking my dog when the incident occurred." I was trying to keep the amount of information I shared to a minimum.

"I heard there was a drug bust going down. Did you know it was going to happen? What about you? You weren't injured, were you?"

"I'm fine. Everything happened very fast. All I know is that Detective Cody was struck by a speeding car. How is she?"

"Still pretty sleepy, but the nurses in the Emergency Department warned me she can be a little cranky. No wonder, though. She has a fracture of her femur, and to quote the x-ray tech 'a totally messed up knee.' Also, some broken ribs, and a scalp laceration."

"That's terrible! But I'm glad she wasn't more seriously injured."

"They're going to have a heck of a time repairing the leg fractures. Hackett is the surgeon, though, and she's the best, so hopefully, there will be a good outcome."

"Thanks for updating me, Jacki."

"No problem. But you know, keep what I told you to yourself. I probably shouldn't have said anything."

It was the way she ended every story that violated patient privacy rights. "Of course!" I said.

Bruno sat patiently at my feet, his red ball in his mouth, asking for a game of fetch. I took him for a quick game in the backyard. It struck me that he seemed to have been more frightened by the police and ambulance sirens than the shots fired by the drug dealers. When we went back inside, I turned on the local news in time to catch the promo before the commercial break. "One man dead, police officer injured in a drug bust gone bad."

I muted the sound as the commercial came on. Of course, they would have to phrase it so it garnered the most attention, but there had been no time for any actual drug bust to occur. Just one dealer and his cohorts against another. Or at least that was what it had seemed to me. The news report came back on, and I hit the button again to un-mute it.

"Local police say twenty-seven-year-old Darren Bourne of New Haven was killed in a drive-by shooting in Madison today. The killing is thought to be related to a dispute between drug dealers. Bourne has a record of arrest related to possession and possession of narcotics with intent to sell. One police officer was injured in the incident but is listed in fair condition at University Hospital. After the break, Hal Mathers will report on how drug violence is creeping into what were once considered our safest neighborhoods."

I turned off the T.V. I didn't need to hear what I had experienced firsthand.

As I was cleaning up after eating a light dinner, I heard a knock at the front door. Bruno ran toward it, his tail wagging. Before I could get there, the door opened, and I heard a voice say softly, "Oh, such a good boy. Come here. Melanie? Are you here?"

"Lynn! You didn't have to stop over. I mean, I'm glad to see you, but really, I'm okay."

"I know you said that, but I thought you might want to talk about it anyway. How is this little guy doing after what happened?" She went over to sit on the sofa and pulled Bruno up into her lap.

"Fine, I think. I was worried he'd regress and go back to some of the behaviors he exhibited after Artie was killed, but so far, he seems okay."

"How about you?"

"I'm still a bit rattled. It seems unreal that I could be involved in something so violent again. A lot like I felt when I found Artie and that woman dead."

"Did you find out anything about Detective Cody's condition?"

I nodded. "She has a broken leg and some broken ribs, but she is stable." I got up to put the tea water on, and Lynn followed me.

"What did Justin say when you told him?"

I suddenly realized that I hadn't called my boyfriend, Justin, to tell him what had happened. I'd met him last summer when he went into practice with Bruno's veterinarian. We'd been dating for three months now and were getting pretty serious. Yet I hadn't thought to call him right away. "Oh, well I haven't told him yet, but…."

"What! Why not?"

"I…don't know. I don't want to sound like a needy female, I guess." I realized how foolish that sounded.

"Do you really believe that's what he'll think?"

"No. I suppose you're right. It's late. I'll call him tomorrow." I figured that would give me some time to tell him about it in such a way that I didn't sound totally reckless.

Lynn sat at the kitchen table while I got out the mugs and milk for our tea. After I poured the tea, I sat opposite her. I realized I hadn't really paid attention to how she looked since she arrived. "Are you all right, you look tired."

"Oh, fine." She gave me a very unconvincing smile. "I am a little worn out. You know, moving and all."

"How are you liking your new place? I need to come over and see it now that you're settled in." Lynn had moved into a condo in a complex bordered by a lake in the neighboring town of Guilford.

"I love being so close to the lake, and the light in the living room is great for my painting. I think it was the right decision to rent instead of buy until I'm sure what I want to do now that I am a free woman." She smiled the same forced smile.

"Okay what's up? Is everything going all right with Doug selling the house in Mesa?"

"Well, it turns out Doug changed his mind. He and his new lady, I mean his new wife, decided to live in the house after all."

"What? What about the money he was going to send after he sold the house?"

"Our lawyers are working out the particulars, but basically, Doug and his new wife will be buying me out." She shook her head. "It is weird, though, to think of some other woman living in my house."

"That is upsetting." I hadn't known Lynn for a long time, but we had been through some intense situations together. She didn't look to me like she was upset, but like she was worried. "I think something else is going on. What is it? I know you're busy with your painting classes, is someone at High Life Dermatology giving you grief?" Lynn had started seeing Alex, the handsome new doctor who had been hired to replace Artie at the dermatology practice. "Is Alex married after all? Gay?"

Her laugh was genuine this time. "Yes, I am busy, between teaching my classes and my job at High Life Dermatology. I also have been invited to show some of my work at an upcoming art show—la de dah. It isn't anything like that."

"So, what is it?"

"There's this guy. He lives at the end of my section at the condo complex."

"Oh? Very interesting...."

She shuddered, "No, nothing like that. As a matter of fact, that's just it. After you helped me move my stuff into the condo, a man came over and asked if I wanted help moving the last box. I thanked him but said I was all set. The guy was pleasant looking, average height, kind of brownish hair, fair complexion, probably in his late thirties I'd say."

I nodded. "Okay. I think I would have been a little hesitant to let someone I didn't know into my house also." Well, I discounted the fact that I had offered to let Lynn, whom I had just met, stay at my house until she could decide if she was going to remain in Connecticut.

"He hung around watching me for a few minutes as I was unpacking my car, and he asked me several more times if I was sure I didn't want help. I said no I was fine, but thanks anyway. He walked away after I turned down his help again, but something about him gave me a bad vibe. I thought it was weird that he was so insistent on helping me into my condo, and now he's around a lot. It seems he's always there when I take a walk along the lake, or when I take the trash to the dumpster. He is staring at me, not saying anything, just watching. It makes me get goose flesh." She rubbed both her arms as if just talking about him gave her the creeps. "Two days ago, I was off, and I decided to take a walk around the lake. It was the middle of the day so most of the other people in my complex were at work and I thought

I'd have the trail to myself. Not long after I started, I heard footsteps behind me. It was him. I figured he routinely walked this time too, so I slowed a bit so he would pass me. He slowed down too and stayed behind me. Maybe I'm just being paranoid, I haven't lived by myself for a while."

I shook my head. "No. I don't think you are being paranoid." Now I felt a ripple of unease on her behalf. "Can you report him to somebody?"

"What can I do? Tell the teacher he's bothering me?" Lynn was the most easy-going person I had met in a long while; it wasn't like her to snap at me. "Sorry, I guess I'm on edge too. You're right. If he steps over any real boundaries, I'll call the police."

"Good. Like you said, let's keep ourselves out of any more trouble. We've had enough."

She got up to leave. "I really am tired, so if you're okay, I think I'll head home."

"Sure. And please text me when you get inside your condo."

She stooped to pet Bruno again before she let herself out, "And by the way, Alex is not gay. And he is very eligible. We are having lunch together tomorrow."

Finding out that someone was stalking Lynn did nothing to decrease the tension I felt after what had happened with Detective Cody that afternoon. I was replaying the whole incident in my mind when my phone rang. I was startled but answered it quickly, thinking it might be Lynn calling to tell me something else.

"Hi. Lynn?" There was no answer, then the call ended. I looked at the display for recent calls and saw it was from "unknown."

When my phone rang again a minute later, I let it go to voicemail.

Chapter Three

After I had taken a hot shower and felt a bit calmer, I checked to see if the second call had been the same unknown caller. The most recent call had been from Justin.

When I called him back, he didn't even give me a chance to explain why I'd missed his call.

"I just saw the news! Please tell me that you weren't anywhere near where that drug dealer was killed today. They said it happened on Windy Reed Road. That's where you walk Bruno sometimes, isn't it?" I could hear the concern in Justin's voice.

Now I felt guilty that I hadn't thought to call him this afternoon. I should have told him before he heard about it on the news. "I'm fine. I didn't want to worry you, so I didn't call you right away, but yes, Bruno and I were there. Detective Cody showed up and wanted to use Bruno as a distraction while she investigated a tip that a drug deal was going to occur. I insisted she take me also. She assured me we would be safe."

I could hear him swear under his breath. "Obviously, that wasn't true. Why would she even ask you to do something like that? And why would you agree to it?"

"In retrospect, I realize it was not a good idea. At the time, she seemed desperate, and as I said, she assured me we would be safe. There were other officers poised to move in to do the actual arrest." I was fighting to keep my own temper under control now.

"A lot of good..."

"I know. I'm sorry if I worried you. But as I've told you, Bruno and I are fine, and Detective Cody is in stable condition."

I could hear him let out a long breath. "I'm sorry. I didn't mean to sound so harsh, but I was frantic. After what happened to you and Bruno over the summer...."

"I understand that. I appreciate your concern, but I'm fine."

He was silent for a moment, "How is Bruno doing? Did the gunshots and commotion cause him to backslide? Anymore 'accidents' or chewing his tail?"

Bruno was sitting in front of me, his stumpy tail wagging, and his tongue out as if he knew who was on the phone and wanted to say hello. I laughed, "No, as a matter of fact, he was far less upset than I was." I hurried to add, "But my nerves have settled now, so stop worrying."

"Okay." He sounded more relaxed now. "How about we go out to Lenny and Joe's for some seafood tomorrow night?"

"Sure. We can go after work . If you don't think it will be too late, maybe we can go for a walk on the beach afterward."

I was glad that we ended our conversation on a good note. I felt bad now about not calling Justin right away and had to think about why I hesitated. I had never found him to be controlling before, or was I reading his reaction wrong?

I was tired, but the excitement of the day made me too keyed up to fall asleep, so I started to scroll through Facebook on my phone. A post caught my eye. It was about how the signs of danger are often dismissed until it's too late. That didn't help. I found myself newly worried about Lynn's situation. I settled for a cup of chamomile tea and sat with Bruno pressed to my hip while I read a nursing journal until my eyes felt heavy.

The next day went quickly since I had a full schedule of patients to see. When it ended, however, I felt satisfied that all my patient visits had gone well, and the thought of seeing Justin later put me in an upbeat mood.

When Justin arrived, he seemed subdued. I was worried that he might bring up my getting involved in dangerous situations again. Instead, he kissed me and said, "No other happenings on the police beat, I hope?"

"Not funny. I really have had my fill of being involved in crime of any sort."

I grabbed my purse and bent over to pet Bruno, who seemed to think he was going to be included in our outing. "Sorry, buddy. You stay and watch the house. I'll be back later."

Despite him trying to joke about the shooting I'd witnessed, I could tell something was bothering Justin. As we drove to the restaurant, at the risk of ruining a meal I'd been looking forward to all day, I asked, "You're not still upset about what happened, are you?"

He shook his head. "I might have overreacted; I'm sorry. It's just that..." He hesitated a moment, then, "I wish you hadn't gotten involved in Detective Cody's case. I'm just glad it worked out all right and you are okay and that it's over now." He took a deep breath. "It's something that happened at the office today. I really shouldn't let it bother me, but I had a patient register a complaint about me. I suggested she use some holistic methods to deal with her dog's anxiety rather than relying on heavy doses of medication. The poor thing was a total slug while I examined him. She said that I didn't know what I was talking about and my suggestions were ridiculous. I heard her insist that she only see Dr. Reddy in the future."

I smiled and rubbed his arm. "No, you shouldn't let it bother you. You were spot on when you prescribed alternative methods to help Bruno with his issues. I'm sure Dr. Reddy will back you up."

We were both quiet for a few minutes. Then Justin said, "I'm sorry, I never even asked how your day was."

"It was a good day. Not one wrong address, so I was able to get to everyone I was supposed to, and there was complete cooperation from everyone I saw."

He smiled, "Great. I'm glad to hear it."

We pulled into the parking lot of the restaurant, and as I opened my car door, the fragrance of fried shrimp and baking scrod made my stomach grumble. "I don't know about you, but I'm starving!" I said.

He laughed and said, "I wasn't sure if that was my stomach or yours."

We were able to get a seat in the rear enclosed porch of Lenny and Joe's Fish Tale, and as I devoured my lobster roll and fries, I watched as the sun set in shades of orange and pink. It would be too late for a walk on the beach after dinner, but I pointed out that we could sit in my front yard and watch the final light over the marshlands across the road from my house.

Once we were settled in my front yard, I went into the house to get Bruno. He immediately jumped up to sit in my lap. The evening was getting cooler, and Justin and I sat side by side, the three of us wrapped in a cozy blanket. We didn't go inside until it was too dark to see anymore.

I put on water for coffee and tea and turned on some music as Justin and I settled on the sofa. I convinced Bruno to sit snuggled on the other side of my hip and had just rested my head on Justin's shoulder when his cell phone rang. He ignored it at first, but after it stopped ringing, it started again almost immediately. He sighed and said, "I better get this."

I was just coming out of the kitchen with our coffee and tea when he ended his call.

"That was a patient who says her cat jumped off the windowsill and caught a claw in the curtain. She says she thinks he ripped a nail out in his left front paw, and she can't stop the bleeding. I told her I'd meet her at the office in fifteen minutes. I'm sorry."

"I understand. Duty calls. You don't have to take emergency calls all the time, though, do you?"

"No. but Dr. Reddy is out of town for a few days, so I said I would cover." He grabbed his jacket, kissed me quickly, and said, "Tomorrow? My place."

I nodded.

As he was about to leave, Justin said, "I nearly forgot. My grandfather wants you to stop over at his house as soon as you get a chance. He thinks he would be bothering you if he called you himself, but it's okay if I am the one to ask you."

Justin's grandfather, Charlie Duggan, was a patient of mine. I laughed. "Is he all right?"

"He's fine. Well, he's himself anyway. He said it's not in your professional capacity, he just wants to speak to you."

"That's intriguing. Do you know what it's about?"

"No. But I am curious as heck. I hope he isn't about to tell you you can do better than me."

"Never." As I shut the door behind him, my own cell phone began to chime. The screen said it was Lynn.

"Hi. I'm at my condo in my car. I just got back from an evening class, and that guy I told you about is outside."

"What is he doing? He isn't approaching your car, is he?"

"No. When I pulled in, I thought he was coming from around my condo, but maybe he was taking something to the dumpster. Now he is just sort of lingering outside his door. It looked like he was watching me from the time I pulled in until I parked my car. Just stay on the phone with me until I get in my door, okay?"

"Of course. But if you say he is coming toward you or anything, I'm hanging up and calling the police."

"No. He is just standing there. I'm almost inside. Okay. Thanks. Sorry to bother you."

"It's not a bother, but maybe you should ask around and see if anyone knows him or has any information about him. It sounds threatening, but maybe there is an explanation for his behavior."

"I guess there could be, but I just keep getting a bad feeling whenever I see him."

I thought back to the piece I'd read online the night before and all the advice I'd gotten in a self-defense class I'd taken. "You're right to trust your gut. I just hope that it turns out that he is annoying but harmless."

After I ended the call with Lynn, I went to check the locks on the doors and peek out the front window. I felt silly. I knew fear could be contagious, but after making the rounds, I did feel better.

Chapter Four

I had the following day off, so decided to stop in and see what Charlie Duggan, Justin's grandfather, wanted. I had been following Charlie for some time for problems related to his type II diabetes, and most recently, after a below-the-knee amputation of his left leg due to complications. According to Justin, however, this was unrelated to Charlie's health.

Charlie answered shortly after I knocked on his front door, something that had rarely happened before. I was glad to see he was wearing his prosthetic leg, as it had taken some time and practice to convince him to do so. "Hello. See my grandson gave you my message. Come on in then." His gait was steady as he led me to the living room.

"Look at you! You are doing wonderfully on your leg," I said.

"Yeah, gettin' used to it." He looked pleased with himself.

His little Pomeranian, Rex, had looked up as I entered but had not vacated his usual spot in the easy chair he occupied. He got up briefly now and turned in a circle, and settled down again as I sat on the sofa next to Charlie.

"Justin said you wanted to see me about something?"

"It's the lady next door. Something ain't right over there."

"What do you mean, not right? How can you tell? Have you been over there?" Next door was a good half acre away from Charlie's small ranch house.

"There's a lady lives there by herself. We say hello, but that's about the extent of it. Her name is Emma. I see her out walking most days. She is no spring chicken, but she always had a vigorous step to her. Couple of days ago, I saw her out walking, and she seemed to be kind of ambling along and turned in circles a couple of times like she was confused or unsure where she was going. She hasn't been walking since. Earlier this week, I heard a commotion over there, must have been midnight or later. I was up watching Colbert on the TV, and I heard a noise, like someone yelling or something. I got up to look, and I could have sworn I saw somebody out there around her house."

I had to admit that sounded like a reason for some concern, but there could be plenty of logical explanations for her not following her daily routine. "Maybe she is away on vacation and had someone watching the house. If she is home, the noise could have been from a loud TV. If you're really worried, you could call the police for a wellness check."

"I done that already. They said they went to the house, and she answered the door herself. Looked to be all in one piece. They said they asked if she was all right, and she said she was."

"Then...."

He shook his head, "I used to be in law enforcement myself, and something tells me something isn't right over there."

Charlie had been a security guard at a local factory before he retired and still liked to keep track of what was going on in both his neighborhood and in the community in general. I had gotten used to the constant murmur and occasional loud announcement from the police scanner he always has on.

"Still, it sounds to me as if you have done what you can, unless you see something else that makes you think she is having trouble."

"I thought of one more thing." He gave me what I swear was a sly look. "My daughter brought me some tomatoes she put up this summer. More than I can use. You could bring her a couple of jars. Tell her I thought she might be able to use them. You got medical knowledge. See if she looks all right to you."

"I don't know, Charlie. What if she doesn't open the door when I knock? Besides, one look isn't going to tell me much unless something is obviously wrong. And I can't just show up in a professional capacity and demand to examine her."

"Well, you talked your way into getting me to open the door more than a time or two."

That made me smile, but I still felt hesitant to barge in on the woman. However, even if I couldn't really tell much by meeting the neighbor on her doorstep, it wouldn't hurt to bring the canned tomatoes to her. Also, it might appease Charlie. Persistence was one of his most endearing, and at times, annoying, qualities.

Ten minutes later, I found myself trudging up to his neighbor's door, two jars of tomatoes in hand. The name on the mailbox was "Reynolds." I rang the bell, and a small white-haired lady dressed in purple sweats answered the door. The fragrance of what I thought must be a stew wafted out after her. I hadn't had lunch yet, and my stomach growled at the aroma.

"Mrs. Reynolds?" She looked to be a spry eighty or so.

"Yes?" She smiled.

I held out the jars of canned tomatoes. "These are from your neighbor, Mr. Duggan. His daughter gave him more than he could use. He said you might be able to use them. I'm...a friend of the family, and he asked me to bring these over to you."

"That's lovely. Please tell Charlie I said thank you. I heard he had surgery a bit ago, is he doing well?"

"Oh yes. He's fine." I figured the best thing to do was just come right out with Charlie's concerns. "He was a little worried about you, though. He hasn't seen you taking your usual walk lately, and he thought he heard a loud disturbance over here the other night." I hoped she wouldn't just tell both Charlie and me to mind our own business.

Instead, she looked a little distressed. "Oh, I'm fine. You know, I'm getting a bit older. I get a little befuddled every now and then. A little rest and I'm good as new. I'll be back to walking soon. The noise was just my grandson and his friends. I forgot and locked my garage door. I said he could keep some of his belongings there until he gets a place of his own." She had been looking directly at me until she came to the end of her explanation. Now she was focusing on something just past my shoulder. "I'm sure they didn't want to disturb the neighborhood."

Her explanation seemed meant to reassure me and get me to leave, but she didn't seem to be in any immediate distress and looked physically well enough. "Good. I'll tell Charlie there isn't reason to worry." I smiled and nodded to her. She nodded back and then rather abruptly shut the door.

When I got back to Charlie's to let him know what Emma Reynolds had said, he'd already put on a kettle of water and had two cups set out with tea bags in them. He paused in the act of retrieving a carton of milk from the refrigerator and turned to look at me shaking his head.

"Huh. Getting older, she said. Well, I'm still keeping an eye and an ear out. And I seen that grandson and his friends and don't think much of them. Family is family, but there's usually some rotten fruit on every tree."

I had sensed something was a bit off, too. But I didn't want to get Charlie any more riled up.

"You got another minute?" He handed me a cup of tea and motioned me toward the sofa again. "Something else I was going to talk to you about."

"Sure." I had a sudden panicked thought that maybe he was going to put in his two cents on my relationship with Justin.

"I heard about what happened the other day; you being there when the guy got shot, and the police officer injured. I got to say, you sure do get involved in some tricky situations for such a quiet-looking young lady."

That came out of left field, and I felt something between hurt and anger. "I don't…., I never meant to get involved…." I took a deep breath. "Didn't you just ask me to check on your neighbor and make sure she was all right?" I thought I'd become used to Charlie's bluntness, and I didn't think I would have been so offended if two other people hadn't recently pointed out my penchant for getting involved in dangerous situations.

Charlie held out his hands as if to appease me. "Guess I didn't say that right. What I was thinking was you got a way of getting to the bottom of things and not panicking when things go wrong. I was wondering if you have any ideas about what was going on with the cop being injured and all."

I could feel my irritation fade away, because I did feel like there was more going on in that whole incident than I had been told. "No. Not really. I did wonder how the other woman and I were able to dodge being hit by the car, but Detective Cody was not. Her reflexes must be as good as ours. Probably better."

Charlie leaned back on the sofa, his tea untouched. "Huh. See, you make a good point." He leaned forward again and looked at me as if something had just occurred to him. "You know, if you learn anything else and want to run any other thoughts you have by somebody, I might be interested to listen."

I fought to suppress a smile. "I'm beginning to think you had other motives for asking me to stop by besides checking on Mrs. Reynolds."

I think he actually started to blush. "Well, I got to do more than sit here all day watching the dang TV." He motioned to his prosthetic leg, "I may not be in any shape to run down the perps anymore, but I still got a few brain cells left."

I smiled. "I never would have questioned that, but I'm not really involved in the shooting or Detective Cody's accident anymore."

He nodded, "I know, but you still got some questions, right?"

I thought a minute before answering. "Yes. But I swore I'd steer clear of dangerous situations from now on."

"All I'm saying is if you have any ideas you want to run by somebody, let me know." He motioned to the police scanner emitting occasional codes and squawks in the background, "I hear anything interesting, and I'll give you a jingle."

Much as I planned to keep my word to stay out of police business, running my questions and thoughts by someone was not going to hurt anything. And Charlie Duggan always had an interesting take on things. "All right. Deal. But we won't get involved in the investigation."

I motioned for him to stay seated as I got up to leave, but he stood up anyway to walk me to the door. "My nurse says I got to keep exercising on this new leg, and she can be a real pain about me following medical orders." He winked at me. "Oh, and let's not tell Justin about our little discussion."

I started to open my mouth to object, but he said, "Not just yet, okay?"

Chapter Five

Judy was smirking as she handed me the paperwork for a new patient Coretrack was scheduled to do follow-up care on. "I saved this one for you. I thought you would be a perfect fit to work with her."

I glanced at the name and address of the patient and gave Judy a startled look. "Really? Detective Cody?"

She nodded, "You have a knack for working with challenging patients. The report from the discharging unit at the hospital on Ms. Cody indicated she was not the easiest person to treat. She has her own ideas about how quickly her recovery should be and seemed to think that medical orders were only suggestions."

I felt conflicted about taking the case. I really wanted to, if for no other reason than I was curious about what was going on in the drug dealer investigation. Maybe I could squeeze some scraps of information from Detective Cody. She would be on pain meds after all. However, I knew that was the very reason I shouldn't take the case. I had too much of an interest in her professional business.

"You do know that I have had dealings with Detective Cody in the past and that I was with her when she was injured? Maybe it wouldn't be ethical to be the one to do her care."

Judy raised her eyebrows, and said, "Do you plan on violating HIPPA laws?"

"No. of course not." Besides, I had a sinking feeling that no matter what state Detective Cody was in, she would never tell me something she didn't want me to know.

"Then I trust you will give her the best care, and unless she has a problem with you being her nurse, I don't see that we have an issue."

I had no trouble finding Detective Cody's house, as I had done several other cases in the neighborhood. I pulled into the driveway behind a yellow Prius.

The door was answered by an older woman with a long gray braid, dressed in a blouse with rolled-up sleeves and a long, flowered skirt. The head of a little girl peeked out from behind her skirt.

I extended my hand, "Hi, I'm Melanie Bass from Coretrack Homecare. I'm here to see Ms.—Detective Cody."

She shook my hand and then stepped aside to let me enter. The little girl clung to her skirt, but she gently guided her out in front of her. "I'm Pauline Moran, Sunny's mother, and this is her daughter. Please come in."

The little girl had huge blue eyes, and the most worried look on her face I'd seen on a child in some time.

I leaned down to speak to her, "And what is your name?"

"Katie." Her voice was soft, and I thought I saw tears welling up in her eyes. "Are you here for my mom? She got hurt at work."

Pauline leaned down and brushed back the girl's hair. "Your mother is going to be fine. Ms. Bass is going to help her get better." Pauline stood up and smiled at me, "Please follow me, Ms. Bass, I'll show you to Sunny's room."

It sounded as if Detective Cody was talking to someone as we approached her room. She was sitting up in bed, a phone pressed to her ear. I thought I heard her say, "Jerk!" before she quickly ended the call and shoved the phone under her pillow as we entered. There were several colorful crayon drawings taped to her nightstand and on the wall around her bed. A flurry of printed pages was strewn around her, and a laptop was open on the bedside table beside her. Her right leg, sporting a large ace bandage and splint, was propped on a pillow. She looked startled when she saw me following her mother and daughter into the room. "What...? Ms. Bass?" She quickly ruffled the papers together, closed the laptop, and placed them face down on top of it. "It was nice of you to check in on me, but you needn't have come all this way."

I took a small perverse pleasure in her being a bit flustered at seeing me. Also, my curiosity peaked at what she had been doing that she didn't want me to see. "Well, it really isn't very far for me to come, and secondly, I'm here officially. My agency, Coretrack Homecare, sent me to follow up on your care. Your doctor is concerned you're not following all his instructions."

A little voice piped up behind me, "Mama are you going to get in trouble for not listening again?"

Cody smiled, "No, honey. I'm listening to everything the doctor said." She gave her mother a challenging look.

"Come on, little miss, let's let Ms. Bass do her work. You can help me make the dough for the bread we're going to bake!" Mrs. Moran reached to take Katie's hand.

"No! I want to stay with Mommy!" She ran over to throw her arms around her mother's neck.

Detective Cody hugged her for a moment, then said, "Katie, you know what would make me feel better? A couple of slices of warm bread. Could you help Nanna make it for me?"

Katie let go of her mother and nodded. "Okay." She went back to stand by her grandmother, and Mrs. Moran led the girl from the room.

Detective Cody cleared her throat, "I never really thanked you for helping me after I was injured. So, thank you."

I smiled and said, "You're welcome. I'm glad you have good enough reflexes to have started to move out of the way before that car hit you more directly."

She looked away from me for a moment, "Yes. Well, I thought I was well out of the way of it. Apparently not."

"Do you think whoever was driving could have hit you intentionally?"

"I don't know. According to Greg Langley, they think the guy driving was high and lost control when shots were fired. I am glad you and your neighbor had the sense to duck and dive, however." She pointed to my medical bag, "What is it you need to do today?"

"I need to take your vital signs and see how your injuries are healing. And make sure you are following doctor's orders." I gave her a meaningful look.

I took out my stethoscope and listened to Detective Cody's breath sounds.

In addition to a fracture of her right leg and knee, she had fractured three ribs, a collapsed right lung, and a laceration of her scalp at the hairline. The cut on her scalp was healing well, and though she said she still had some pain with deep breathing due to her ribs, her breath sounds were clear and equal now. I took the earpieces of my stethoscope from my ears. "Your daughter is adorable. How old is she?

"Four. A very old four."

"Her name is Katie?"

"Katherine Anne. Having grown up with a name like Sunshine Meadow, you can see why I chose to go with a more traditional name." She pulled herself up straighter in bed and gave me an embarrassed look. "My parents were living in a commune when I was born. It could have been worse, I guess. There was a Peace, Love, and a Wonderweed born while they were there."

I chuckled and said, "I hate to tell you, but those aren't even the most unusual names I've heard." I paused for a moment, "Katie seems very upset about what happened to you."

"That's why I need to get up and back to normal as soon as possible. Right now, I'm doing all I can to reassure her I'm okay." I noticed she didn't look at me as she spoke.

"Maybe it would help her to talk to someone about..."

"No. I have this. She'll be all right."

I had the feeling Detective Cody had heard all she wanted to on the subject. I continued to check her vital signs. "Your heart rate is a little elevated, and you have a low-grade temp. Do you have any pain in the incision in your leg?"

"No. I'm fine."

"I'm worried you might have a wound infection. The incision needs to heal before the doctor can put a cast on it. Have you been taking all your antibiotics?"

"Yes. As I said, I am following doctor's orders." She shifted her weight again in bed but winced as she did so.

"You haven't been putting any weight on it, have you? Let me just have a look and make sure the incision looks okay."

She hesitated a moment, but then said, "Okay. But, really, it's fine."

I unwrapped the ace bandage from around her wound and removed the gauze covering it. The lower end of the incision looked clean and had no drainage, but the upper border was reddened with thick drainage oozing from it, and the sutures were pulled taut. I looked at her and pointed to the area I was concerned about. "It looks like an area of infection may be starting here. The doctor will need to look at this. She may have to release the sutures over that area."

"I'll call the doctor and see if she wants to see you today and if she wants to extend the course or switch antibiotics. How about pain meds?" I asked.

She shook her head, "I don't like taking narcotics. I took one the day I was discharged, and I was fuzzy-headed the entire day. Over-the-counter pain relievers are enough."

The mention of narcotics made me glance toward the sheaf of papers she had stashed on her bedside table. "I thought the doctor's instructions also included rest." I motioned toward the table. "Do those have to do with the case you were working on when you got hurt?"

She looked annoyed for a moment. "Not officially. Technically, I've been replaced on the team since I'm not mobile for the time being." She motioned to her leg. "But I got permission to 'unofficially' help out. I've been working on this for over a year, and I'll be damned if I'm going to be pushed out now."

"I heard the man who was killed was a known drug dealer."

"He was. But he also was the informant who tipped us off that the drug deal was going to occur that afternoon. He was trying to get a reduction in charges for some of the crimes he was wanted on. Also, he...never mind."

I thought about how I had waved to the man as we approached the car and felt a surge of guilt. I wondered if the others involved took that as an indication that we knew him, and that helped get him killed. I didn't remind Detective Cody of my faux pas, but instead asked, "Was your team able to find the second car?"

"Not yet. I didn't get any identifying information before he hit me, so we don't have much to go on other than we all agree it was a light-colored medium-size sedan."

"I'm sorry, I didn't get a good look at it either in all the confusion."

Detective Cody sighed, "Too bad. Who was the woman with the dog we met when we approached the parked car? Why was she there?"

"That was a neighbor who lives a couple of houses down from me. It seems like we're often walking our dogs there around the same time. I don't really know her. As a matter of fact, I remembered her dog's name was Shiloh, but I forgot her name until she told me after the incident."

"So, what was her name? You said she told you after the shooting?"

I thought it was telling that she focused on the shooting instead of the fact she was nearly turned into roadkill. "It's Audrey Cullen. But your colleagues got her name when they interviewed her. They didn't share that info with you?"

"No. They seem to think I can't heal and work at the same time." She jotted something on the back of one of the papers she had stacked on her laptop. "How was she acting after what happened?"

"A bit in shock, unsure what we had just witnessed. Much the way I felt, I guess. As I said, Detective Cody..."

"Why don't you just call me Sunny? I am totally at the mercy of your care right now; I don't think we need to be so formal."

I nodded, "First names it is, then."

"In any case, if you remember anything or hear anything you think might be significant, you can give me a call."

I raised one eyebrow and said, "It sounds as if you are doing a lot of work for someone who is supposed to rest."

"Just trying to keep my mind busy. Besides, as I said, I haven't been forbidden to work." Then she murmured, "Not yet anyway." She looked right at me, opened her mouth as if to say something, then changed her mind.

"Did you have a question?"

"I seem to remember you're pretty good at nosing around. I was just going to ask if you could speak to your neighbor, see if she remembered anything else about that day. Sometimes people think of things a few days after the incident."

I let her crack about being nosy pass, mostly because it was true. "Okay, I can do that."

So much for staying out of police business, but Sunny had asked, and it only involved asking a question or two.

I wasn't sure how to approach Audrey, but I'd figure something out. I packed up my blood pressure machine and stethoscope and put them into my bag. Then I put in a call to Sunny's orthopedic surgeon and made an appointment for later that day. "Will your mother be able to get you to your appointment later?"

She nodded.

"Is there anything else I can do for you before I go?"

She leaned forward and grabbed the crutches propped next to the bed. "If you wouldn't mind, could you help me get up onto these? I need to use the bathroom. I'm getting the hang of the walking, but up and down is still very undignified."

I helped her get steady on her crutches, but she waved me away as she lurched toward her bathroom. I looked around as I waited for her to come out. I looked longingly at the papers she had put aside but decided not to cross that privacy line. On her dresser were two photos in frames: one of her several years younger, with a newborn baby in her arms, the other of a handsome man in a police uniform. He was beaming ear to ear. I heard the door behind me open.

"Me with Katie when she was one day old. The other is my husband, Brian." Sunny began a slow wobble back toward her bed.

I walked beside her just in case she started to pitch over. "In the picture with your daughter you have that new mother look of both joy and fright."

"True. I think that feeling never really goes away."

"Your husband is a police officer also?"

"He was. He's deceased. Shot while trying to stop a known drug dealer from breaking into an electronics store after dark. We had a good lead on the guy who we think did it, but before he could be arrested, his body was found in an alley in New Haven. Drug overdose complicated by a bullet to the chest."

"I'm sorry. I remember reading about that case in the local paper. I never made the connection to you until now." I had a strong suspicion that I knew now why Sunny's daughter seemed so worried about what happened to her mother.

Sunny grunted as she settled against her bed, "Brian was a good cop. A careful cop. He never would have tried to apprehend that guy by himself under those circumstances."

"Are you saying that you don't believe it happened the way it appeared?"

She handed me her crutches. "I don't believe the report tells the whole story. You ever hear the expression 'cover your ass'?"

I propped her crutches where she could reach them, and I helped her lift her injured leg onto the bed. Once I got her settled in a comfortable position again, I said, "What about your department? Have you told them about your doubts?"

She compressed her lips and shook her head. "Many times. I was told all the evidence was reviewed, and there seemed no reason to change the report as to how Brian was killed. His killer reaped his just rewards. End of story."

"I'm sorry." I didn't know what else to say. I had been involved in a similar, but less serious incident when I worked at University Hospital. I felt my concerns were not being addressed either.

"So. What now?" She motioned to her leg.

"I'll talk to Dr. Hackett after she sees you this afternoon and find out what her plan is for you now. I'll be back to check on you in two days. In the meantime, be sure to continue to follow all the doctor's instructions."

She mumbled something to herself, but then looked at me with a forced smile. "I will. Thank you." As I walked out of her bedroom door, I saw her reach for her laptop again.

I was about to let myself out when Katie came out of the kitchen. The front of her shirt and jeans were covered in flour. "I helped Nanna like mommy asked. We have to let the dough rise, but you can stay and have some after it's baked."

"Good job! But I need to go for now. Maybe you could save me a piece for the next time I come to see your mom."

She nodded, then looked up at me and said, “Is my mom gonna die?”
I felt my own eyes well up. “No. She isn’t.”

Chapter Six

I took advantage of the mild weather the following day to get some yard work done. Bruno was especially spunky, running around our small backyard, burrowing into the leaf piles I was making as I raked. He seemed happy, and was getting a lot of his energy out, but I was feeling restless myself. I kept thinking of what Sunny Cody had asked me to do the previous day. I hadn't taken Bruno on a walk past the tidal marsh since the day of the shooting. We had limited our walks to going to Hammonasset Beach State Park, or around the downtown area, walks we both loved, but which required a short car ride.

"Okay, little buddy, come on, we need to walk for a while." I brought him into the house and grabbed his leash. "We will not let what happened the other day ruin our special place, will we?" I realized I was repeating an affirmation for myself.

As we approached the point where the paved road ended, and the dirt and gravel road began, I took a deep breath. I had faced down bad memories many times before. When I worked at the hospital, it often was the room where a patient I'd grown close to had died, and certainly in the past months when I passed the highway rest stop where I found my ex, Artie, murdered. I concentrated on the yellows and reds of the trees in the wooded area to my left, I saw an egret fly up out of the sea grass and reeds, and I was able to wipe the vision of Detective Cody lying in the road and the dead man in the water from my mind. At least for a bit.

As we got further along the road, Bruno's tail started to wag frantically, and I spotted Audrey Cullen and her dog, Shiloh, approaching from the other direction. She was fighting to keep him from dragging her along; his tongue was out, and he was leaping up, and dancing on his hind legs in an expression of pure joy and energy. It was something that seemed to be his perpetual state each time we met them.

"Hi." I waved to Audrey as she approached with Shiloh. I realized this was my opportunity to ask her if she remembered anything else about the cars or the people in them on the day of the incident.

"Hi." Her greeting was tentative, but then I saw a look of recognition on her face. "I see you're back to walking your dog here too."

"Yes. I figured since I always loved this walk, it wasn't fair to let what happened ruin it for me."

She nodded but didn't look at me. She petted Shiloh, trying to calm him as he danced around Bruno.

I cleared my throat, "So much of what happened that day is a blur. I just remember seeing you chasing Shiloh and then being afraid of being hit by that car. Do you remember anything else about what happened?"

She shook her head, "Not really. Shiloh just suddenly yanked the leash out of my hands and took off. I got a quick look at the car as it sped past me. I couldn't believe some jerk was going so fast on a dirt and gravel road. Later, I thought the speeding light-colored car might have looked familiar, but I wasn't sure."

"Where was it you thought you saw it before?" I felt my heart rate pick up.

She took a beat or two to answer, as if she was deciding what to say. "It was kind of a non-descript car. I'm probably wrong. It sort of looked like a car that I saw one of my son's friends driving."

"Did you tell the police this?"

"No. Like I said, I didn't think of it until later, and I couldn't be sure it was the same car."

I tried to keep all judgment out of my voice. "But why didn't you mention it to the police when you thought of it?" If my son hung out with whoever was in that car, I'd want to know right away. "Do you know his friend's name?"

She shook her head, "No. Besides, I don't want to get some poor kid in trouble for something he had no part in. Those kids are sometimes a little reckless, but they would never be involved in a real crime or anything." There was no mistaking the defensive note in her answer. "You said you're not a cop, right?"

"No. I'm a nurse. I work for a home care agency." I didn't mention that I was supposed to be keeping my eyes and ears open for any info that might interest someone who *was* a cop. "You could be right; it wasn't an uncommon-looking car." I figured it would be easier to get any information out of her if I didn't shut her down with a self-righteous attitude. "I never asked, how old is your son? You said the other day he plays soccer?"

Her shoulders relaxed a little. "Tyler is sixteen. He's captain of his team. They're prepping to play in the state championship."

"You must be so proud."

She said, "Yes, his father and I...OOOPs!" A squirrel darted across the road about six feet from where we were standing. Shiloh leapt up and yanked her into the brush after it. The squirrel ran up a tree, and it took a few minutes before Audrey was able to wrestle Shiloh back onto the road. "Sorry. I need to go; he's better if we keep moving." She waved and took off down the road before I could ask her any more questions.

Unless Audrey suddenly remembered where she had seen the car and who it belonged to, it wasn't going to be much help in Sunny Cody's investigation. As we passed the area where Sunny Cody, Bruno, and I first saw the parked car two weeks ago, I flashed back to seeing the light-colored car careening towards us, the sound of gunfire, and the thud of Sunny being hit by the car.

"Come, Bruno, over here." I led Bruno toward where Darren Bourne had tumbled down the bank toward the water below. I searched the marsh grass to see if I could find some clue or other useful information hiding there. I realized it was probably a foolish idea since I assumed the police had already thoroughly gone over the area. I progressed from the tall sea grass at the bottom of the bank to the mudflats beyond it. The day Bourne was shot, the tide had been high, and the water came right up to the base of the bank. Today the tide was low, and the sticky mud, rocks, and half-buried shells were exposed. I got excited when Bruno began to sniff and bark at something in the mud, but it turned out to be a small crab. I was about to scramble back up the bank when something farther out in the shallow water and reeds caught my attention. It was dark blue and looked like a piece of partially submerged clothing. I told Bruno to stay and grabbed a thin branch lying near the sea grass. Kicking off my sneakers, I waded out through the shallow water and reeds until I could snag it with my stick. As I pulled it closer, I saw that it was a ball cap.

I was climbing back up the bank, ball cap in hand, when Bruno began to bark frantically at something on the road. I could see the top of a dark-colored vehicle and hear the crunch of gravel as it pulled away. When we got back onto the road again, there were deep tire impressions where a car had pulled onto the verge at the place where we had gone down the bank. There were also footprints where it appeared someone had stood looking down toward the tidal marsh.

I felt a shiver wash over me. I wasn't sure if it was caused by the cool air on my wet pant legs, or the idea that someone might have been watching me. "Come on, Bruno, let's go." I held the hat by two fingers far away from my body as we walked home. I was fairly sure the cap Darren Bourne wore that day was blue.

Once I'd changed into dry clothes, I looked at the hat again. It was stained with sea salt, but it was a faded navy blue. My guess was that if it was the one Bourne was wearing the day he was killed, it must have flown off his head into deeper water after he was shot. The police searching the area might not have seen it if it sank, but it was more visible today now that the tide was low. The cap itself looked unremarkable. However, I checked the inside and noticed some writing above the sweatband. It looked like it might have once been some kind of list, but the letters were now washed out and faded. I couldn't make sense of whatever had once been written there. The cap was still damp, so I left it out back on my patio until it dried, then I put it on the back seat of my car near a bag of clothing I planned to donate. I decided to bring the ball cap to Sunny Cody when I saw her next and let her decide if it was any help to her case.

Chapter Seven

I thought about what Detective Cody said about the death of her husband as I prepared to head out to my first appointment the next day. We both shared the experience of having a husband murdered. Although in my case, Artie was my ex-husband, and I was not in love with him any longer. Still. I had some sense of the shock and pain she must have felt. My thoughts were interrupted by the sound of my phone.

"Hi." It was Lynn. I was wondering if you had time to meet for lunch today?"

"I am on my way to see a patient now, but I should be able to meet you at noon. Where?'

She named a small restaurant in Guilford that she liked.

I gathered my work bag, purse, and computer and was heading out the door when I saw a man with a black ski mask over his face rifling through my car. The driver's side and rear passenger side doors were open. Bruno immediately began to bark furiously and tried to dart past me, but I was able to stop him before he got out.

I closed the door behind me and without thinking, rushed toward the figure. "Hey! What do you think you're doing?" The man turned and stepped toward me and gave me a hard shove. I went flying backward and landed on my backside. Without saying a word, he grabbed something from my back seat and ran off down the road. I heard a car start and pull away quickly.

It took me a minute to recover, but as soon as I got my bearings, I retrieved my phone and called 911.

While I waited for an officer to arrive and take my statement, I searched my car to see what he had taken. The center console was open, and its contents scattered around the front seat, but I saw that the handful of loose change I had thrown in my cup holder was still there. The only things I could tell that were missing were a bag of clothes bound for the donation bin at church and the navy-blue hat I'd found.

A few minutes later, I listened contritely as Officer Garcia lectured me about the necessity of locking my car. "There has been a rash of car break-ins all along the shoreline. It appears juveniles are being used by an organized crime gang to go into unlocked cars. They are looking for any money or valuables that they can grab quickly. Whatever it is they took, it wasn't worth getting hurt to protect it. You shouldn't have approached the thief."

"I know, but I was so shocked and angry at seeing him in my car I didn't think about what could happen. I'm surprised he didn't take the change, though."

"Maybe you interrupted him before he had a chance to grab it. You're just lucky you weren't seriously injured. Next time just call us."

With that, he nodded to me and left.

Somehow, I had ended up feeling like the one in the wrong here. I could still feel the force that was behind the push I'd received, and I thought that the thief seemed not only bigger but more muscular than a teenager.

I had to readjust all my scheduled visits for the day, as well as lunch with Lynn, due to the morning's excitement. By the time I met Lynn for lunch, two hours later than our original plan, I was starving.

I searched Lynn's face after we were seated and was glad to see that she looked more rested and less tense than the last time I saw her.

"So. Anything new going on at the office?" While I no longer had any connection to High Life Dermatology since my ex-husband, one of the founding partners, was killed, I still was curious about what was going on with the people I knew there.

"Things are starting to get back to normal, I guess. Dr.'s Wang and Devlin told me to give you their best when I saw you. Dr. Harwick's sister is in remission for now, so she is starting to come back part-time. And...."

I smiled and stopped her there. "That's good, but you know what I really want to know. How are things with Dr. Drover? Do your co-workers know you have been seeing each other?"

Lynn sipped her water, a mischievous glint in her eyes. "It's going great. Alex thinks that for the time being, we should be discrete, but I have no doubt there is plenty of gossip going around about the two of us."

We stopped talking for a moment as our lunches arrived. As soon as our server walked away, Lynn asked, "How about you and Justin? Was he upset when you told him about what happened with Detective Cody?"

"In a word, yes. I appreciate his concern, but I think I have proven my ability to take care of myself." I didn't mention that I had somehow let myself be pulled into the investigation of the crimes on Windy Reed Road. I didn't even want to think about what he would say about my approaching the car burglar.

"I don't disagree, but look on the bright side: he cares enough to worry, even if it makes you feel a little smothered."

"I know, and honestly, if he wasn't at least a little worried about me, I'd be upset. It's just that I think he is overreacting a little. Or maybe I'm just being overly sensitive. How about you? What did Alex think about the guy who is stalking you at your condo complex?"

Lynn looked down, pushing a forkful of coleslaw around her plate. "I haven't mentioned it to Alex yet. I don't want to look...okay, I get your point."

"Is the guy still watching you?"

She shrugged. "Yesterday before work, I glanced out my front window, and he was crouched down, tying his sneaker. I thought it odd he picked that place to do it. I wouldn't call him a stalker, but I admit I get a creepy feeling when I get home after dark, and I keep looking behind me when I am taking a walk. I did wait until he continued out of sight before I went out to my car." She paused for a moment, then said, "This morning I got a text, a number I didn't recognize, it said, "Don't paint yourself as something you are not." Maybe it was a mistake, or an ad for something, but it freaked me out a little."

I leaned across the table toward her, "Lynn- this guy's a stalker. Normal behavior does not cause people to feel threatened or uncomfortable in going about their daily lives."

"I guess you are right. But I still don't feel I have grounds to call the police or anything. Maybe I should just confront him. I do have self-defense training, after all."

She must have read the horrified look on my face because she laughed and said, "Just kidding. I remember how little good it did me a few months ago, when I ended up duct taped and semi-conscious in the front seat of my car."

"If you call the police, at least they will have it on record. If he does anything else, they will certainly respond."

Chapter Eight

My patient list the following day indicated I was to check on an eighty-two-year-old woman named Emma Reynolds. The name seemed familiar, and when I checked the address, I realized it was the neighbor Charlie Duggan had been concerned about. Her chart said she had fallen and fractured her arm, and when she came in to have it set, her blood pressure was discovered to be abnormally high. Her primary physician had prescribed medication for her and wanted me to check her blood pressure and general well-being.

The woman who answered the door did not seem like the same feisty octogenarian who I met the previous week. She was dressed appropriately, and I could attribute her slightly mussed white bob to a result of having been roused from a nap, but her pale color and the dull look in her eyes made me concerned.

"Hello, Mrs. Reynolds. I'm Melanie Bass, the nurse from Coretrack Homecare. I've come to check on how you're doing with your new medication."

I could see the look of recognition come into her eyes, "Weren't you here before? You said you were a friend of Charlie Duggan."

Well, at least she still seemed mentally sharp. "That's right, but I'm also a nurse. Dr. Warton wanted me to check on you and see how you are doing."

"Yes. That's right; his office called me to say you'd be coming by." She opened the door wider to let me in.

I watched her walk back toward her living room, where she bid me sit down. Her gait was slow, as if she was unsure of each step. "How have you been feeling? Do you feel dizzy?"

She rubbed her casted arm. "No. Not dizzy."

"Does your arm hurt?" I got out my blood pressure cuff.

"No, my arm is okay. A little itchy under the cast. I've been taking some over-the-counter pain reliever for any pain."

Her blood pressure was well within the desired range; I had been worried that it would be low, causing her unsteadiness. "It says in your chart you broke your arm in a fall. Is that right?"

She chuckled softly, "Yes, I tripped over the darn cat. She always knows when it's dinner time and was coming to let me know."

I hadn't noticed the ginger cat huddled under a side table until then. I smiled, "Yes, I have a dog who also knows when it's time to eat and never lets me forget it. Are you having more trouble with your balance lately? Maybe the medication Dr. Wharton prescribed..."

For the first time, a spark came to her eyes, though I thought it was one of anger. "No. I said I'm fine. Just clumsy, with the help of Pancake here." The cat had come to rub against her ankles.

As she reached down to pet the cat, her sleeve pulled up a little, and I noticed several bruises on her right arm and the back of her hand.

She must have seen me looking, and said, "Like I said before, I'm not as graceful as I once was. Seem to keep knocking my hands against the counter and whatnot. I'm still steady, though. I do fine."

I nodded but said, "I'm just concerned. I want to make sure you don't have another more serious fall. Are you able to see clearly?'

"Like a hawk. If you look in my records, you'll see I've had cataract surgery, and all that was taken care of."

I was about to suggest some sort of support might help her balance but she waved toward the corner of the room. "I have a cane, but I found it only slowed me down. I'm fine on my own as long as Pancake doesn't do a dance around my ankles." She gave me a smile I figured was meant to reassure me, but I planned on recording my concerns in my nursing notes.

She rose and seemed a bit steadier as she escorted me to the door, but like the last time I visited her at Charlie's request, she seemed eager to get me to leave.

I had to agree with what Charlie had said the previous week. Based on her appearance and manner when I first met her, Emma Reynolds seemed "not right." The problem was she did not seem to want help or even admit that she might have a problem.

"Mrs. Reynolds, I agree that you are doing okay on your own, but I wonder if you have any family who live locally who might be willing to pop in and check on you once or twice a week?" I could see her immediately stiffen. "You know, just until your arm is healed and you are feeling back to normal."

"No. I don't need to bother anybody to come over here to babysit me." She opened the door for me and stepped back. "Thank you for stopping by."

I was literally in the neighborhood and had an hour before my next appointment, so I decided to drop in and see Charlie. I wasn't sure if I should say anything about what I learned from Detective Cody. I knocked on the door, and then knowing the usual routine he put people through before he opened it, I popped my head in and called, "Mr. Duggan? Charlie, it's me. Melanie Bass."

He was seated on the sofa, his prosthetic leg on the floor in front of him, and a police procedural opened in his hand. "Remind me to lock that door when you leave."

I blushed a little, not sure if I was welcome after all. "Sorry. I was in the neighborhood and just thought I'd come to say 'hello.'"

"PFFT! I'm glad to see you. Just meant I must be slipping to leave my front door unlocked. Lot of brazen criminals around now—even here where you used to be able to leave your car unlocked and your door wide open all day and night."

His dog, Rex, got up to sniff me briefly and then went back to his spot in an easy chair. "Any good?" I motioned to the book he was reading.

"Not bad. I hate it though when they make the security guard out to be some kind of dimwit."

Charlie had been a security guard for over thirty years. I sat next to him on the sofa. "Is your leg bothering you?"

"It's fine. Took off my shoe, so took off the other too. That's not why you stopped in, is it?"

"No. You're right." I was trying to figure out how much I could say without revealing things about Emma Reynolds that were confidential. "I've been to see your neighbor, Mrs. Reynolds. Do you remember you called me about her last week?"

He glared at me, "Nothing wrong with my memory. What's this got to do with anything? She okay?"

"Yes. Sorry, I can't go into details, but I was wondering if she ever mentioned having family in the area."

"I'm not that close to her to have asked, and when I did talk to her, she never said."

"You said you have seen the grandson. Do you know how old he is?"

Charlie made a sour face, "Old enough to drive by with obnoxious music blasting. Why are you asking?"

"I was wondering if he might be able to keep an eye on her."

"Ha! No. Doesn't seem to stay long when he's there; I hear him roaring away after a few minutes. I can't speak for her, but if it was me, I wouldn't want to be relying on someone like that. Besides, I ain't heard him stopping by in a while."

I would check her chart and see who she listed as emergency contacts. Maybe our social worker or her doctor could convince Mrs. Reynolds to let me or one of our home health aides check on her a couple of times a week if she didn't want to contact her family.

Charlie cleared his throat, "You hear anything else about that drug deal gone wrong you were involved in? Don't suppose you know how that injured cop, Detective Cody, is doing?"

I hesitated for a moment, I didn't want to violate any patient privacy rights, but I was curious to hear what Charlie might make of the few bits of information I had been able to gather. "I saw her a few days ago, and she is healing. She is stubborn, though, and insists on continuing to work on the case from home even though she is supposed to be letting someone else handle the investigation while she is recovering." I didn't add that she reminded me of someone else whose care I was involved in.

"Can't say I blame her. Being run down like that, I'd want to be the one to get to the bottom of it myself."

"Detective Cody asked me to speak to my neighbor who was there when the shooting happened. She wanted to know if she remembered anything else about the car or maybe saw someone in either car. I ran into my neighbor when I was walking Bruno and brought the incident up. She said that the car that hit Detective Cody might be similar to one she's seen driven by one of her son's friends, but she isn't sure. She hasn't mentioned this to the police. I'll tell Detective Cody and see what she says."

He nodded, "Yep. And you can bet if your neighbor told you that little bit she is keeping something else she noticed back. Or something she suspects or is worried about."

I had a feeling he was right. "I have to get to my next appointment, but can I get you anything before I leave?" I stood up and gave Rex a final pat.

"Nah. Thanks for stopping in, though. Next time, come when you can stay a bit and bring that grandson of mine with you."

"I will." As I let myself out, I said, "I'll turn the lock for you."

Chapter Nine

I had promised Lynn I would come and see her new condo now that she was finally all settled in. Bruno danced around my legs as I took his leash from the hook by the door. If I had ever considered leaving him at home the look he gave me as I gathered my things would have changed my mind. "Come on, we are going to see Auntie Lynn!" He hopped into the back seat as soon as I opened the rear door, and I buckled him into his car restraint.

It was a pleasant ride up to the complex where Lynn was living. The trees were in full fall color and the sun reflected off the water in the lake near the complex. I found her condo with no trouble, and as Bruno and I walked from the visitor parking space Lynn came out to greet us.

After we did a quick embrace, she bent to scratch under Bruno's chin. "How's this good boy? I have a special treat inside for you!" She looked up at me, "If that is all right with you."

"Of course. How could I refuse."

I loved how Lynn had decorated her new space. The picture of a desert landscape she had painted for Artie was hanging on the wall over a side table as you entered, but the rest of the spacious open floor plan was decorated in blues and green, with seashell and nautical prints covering her furniture and throw pillows. A spiral staircase led up to her sleeping loft, and I noticed she had hung two of her small paintings of the marsh opposite my house on the wall near the staircase. She said, "I decided it was time to leave the past behind. A new place, a new theme. I didn't overdo it did I?"

"No. I really like it. It looks...peaceful."

"Good. That is what I was going for. As I said—a fresh start."

Lynn made butternut squash soup and turkey sandwiches for us and gave Bruno a bacon doggie treat as we sat down to eat.

"So. Have you found out any more about your stalker?" I asked between bites.

"It creeps me out when you call him that. I did receive a weird note in the mail the other day. It was mailed, but there was no return address. She got up and retrieved it from her counter and handed it to me.

"I know about you and what you are doing! Stop now! It will not be tolerated!"

I handed it back to her. "That's scary. Maybe you should hand that over to the police. Tell them about this guy you think is stalking you."

"I thought about it, but then I really don't know what they mean. What if it's from a neighbor who doesn't like the way I separate my recyclables from the garbage or something. I'll hang onto it, and if I get any more notes, I'll bring them to the police."

I wasn't sure her plan was the best one. However, I couldn't make her report the man to the police.

"Have you asked around to see if any of your neighbors know who he is?"

"I asked the woman who lives next door, and she didn't know anything about him except that he just recently moved in also. She said that according to her friend, who is employed by the realty company, the owners are leasing it to him short term while they are out of the country."

That sounded a little suspicious. I didn't say anything to Lynn, but I could tell by the look she gave me that she was having similar thoughts.

"Does he work, do you know? Have you ever seen him leaving around the same time of day or anything?"

"No, but to tell you the truth, I am trying not to pay any attention to him at all. I haven't seen him in a couple of days, and I'm hoping he has given up on any interest he had in me."

"Maybe. That would be the best solution."

Lynn gathered up our lunch dishes and placed them in the dishwasher. "So, how is it having our buddy Detective Cody as a patient? Does she cooperate at all with the instructions she's been given?"

I chuckled, "She is very stubborn, but I have to say she has been quite cooperative with her care. Her stubbornness may work to her advantage as she is determined to get back the normal use of her leg and go back to work. She, of course, is trying to work even as she is supposed to be recovering."

"Did she let slip any information she has about what was going on that day? Or is she still insistent that 'this is our job, Miss Bass; you just mind your own business'?"

I didn't say anything, just gathered Bruno up onto my lap as I thought about how to answer and how much of Sunny's personal history to share.

Lynn slapped the table lightly, "No! She really let you in on what's going on?"

"She did tell me a little bit, she certainly isn't sharing everything about the case, but she asked me to speak to my neighbor Audrey Cullen again to see if she can remember anything else about that day."

"I remember us talking about keeping ourselves out of dangerous situations from now on," she said.

"This isn't dangerous, I just needed to ask a few questions, and now I'm going to relay the answers."

"Hmmm. Well, just so long as you don't get drawn deeper into another police investigation, that may be true." Lynn stood up and glanced out her kitchen window as if checking for someone. Then turned to face me, a grin on her face. "But if you do, make sure you let me know—I've got your back."

I thanked Lynn for the lunch and, assuring her I loved how she had decorated her place, snapped Bruno's leash on again as I prepared to leave.

Lynn grabbed a light jacket and said, "It's such a gorgeous day. I'll walk you both to the car."

Once we were outside, I could see Lynn looking around, and I found myself also scanning the area for suspicious-looking men, even though I had no idea what her presumed stalker looked like. I said, sotto voce, "You don't see him, do you?"

"No. It's been a few days since I've seen him watching me, I keep telling myself I can probably relax now."

I nodded and gave Lynn a brief hug.

I backed out of my spot, and then Bruno and I watched as Lynn walked back to her front door and waved goodbye.

Chapter Ten

When I went to check on Detective Cody the next day, she answered the door herself. She stood to the side of the door leaning on her crutches and then quite gracefully pivoted and walked back a few paces to allow me to enter.

"Wow, I didn't expect you to be the one to greet me."

"Katie is at pre-K, and my mom needed to go home for a few things and to check that my dad hadn't burned down the house or anything. I'm getting pretty good on these things, and I keep telling her she doesn't need to stay with me anymore, but she won't listen."

"How is Katie doing?"

"Okay. A few episodes of temper tantrums at school, but she's four, so it's not that unexpected, right?"

I hesitated to bring up again that her daughter may be having a tough time with what happened to her. Especially since she'd lost her father a couple of years before.

Sunny led me into the living room, where I could see her laptop set up on the coffee table. There were papers spread out next to it, and a few had fallen to the floor. I motioned toward her setup and said, "Still getting a lot of rest, I see."

She eased down onto the sofa in front of the coffee table, positioning her right leg under the table. "This is rest. At least to me." She reached toward the fallen papers, but a few had drifted under the coffee table, and she couldn't grasp them.

"Here. Let me." As I gathered up the four or five pages, I noticed the name "Darren Bourne" scrawled in the column beside one paragraph and underlined three times. I still wondered if I had given him away as a police informer by seeming to know him, and I felt at least partially guilty for his death.

"Did Mr. Bourne identify who the men were that were supposed to supply the drugs that day?"

Sunny reached for the papers, but as I was handing them to her, one slipped from her grasp. As I picked it up again, I saw it looked like a police form, and another name popped out at me: "Brian Cody."

Sunny looked at me as I gave her the form and just said, "Thanks." She replaced the paper in the pile on the table. "Bourne did give us two names. We have a BOLO on Reno Kemp. The other guy he named, Leo Johnson, was not one of the men there that day. He was in Bridgeport Hospital with a stab wound at the time. Bourne didn't mention that there would be a third guy."

I sat opposite her in an easy chair and placed my work bag on the floor. "I'm sorry things went so wrong that day when you asked for my help. I still feel a little responsible for Mr. Bourne's death."

Sunny leaned back against the back of the sofa; I noticed her wince a bit as she did so. "First of all, I didn't ask for your help. I asked to borrow your dog, and you insisted you tag along. Secondly, I'm pretty sure Bourne wasn't shot because he led us to some small-time drug dealers. I think he had some information related to something else. Something someone did not want him to reveal."

I had seen her husband's name on one of the papers. "I remember you said that you thought there was more to your husband's death than was reported. Do you think Bourne knew something?"

She gathered the scattered papers into a pile and set them by her laptop. "I don't know for sure what he knew. I'm just trying to satisfy myself that when Brian was killed, it happened the way it was reported." She looked at me, "You know what it's like to have questions about how and why someone was killed."

"Yes." I didn't add that in my case, though, I had reason to look into it whether I wanted to or not. "And you think Bourne may have provided a link to what happened."

"Maybe." She straightened the papers in front of her. "I got a cryptic message saying I should be there when that drug deal happened, that he could provide me with some interesting information. That's one reason I was there."

"But he never got a chance to speak to you." I felt a twinge of blame again, but I knew she was right that it wasn't my fault he was killed. "Before anything could happen, though, that car came speeding...."

"And hit me."

I had a feeling that we were both thinking the same thing. "Maybe Bourne wasn't the only target."

"I told myself that maybe the driver was high like the report said or that the driver was startled by the shots fired. I no longer think that is the case."

"I went back to the spot where Mr. Bourne was shot, and I found something."

She sat up straight. "What?"

"I noticed something caught in the reeds offshore. I snagged it, and it turned out to be his ball cap. There was some sort of writing in it, but whatever it was had become too washed out and smeared by the water for me to make any of it out."

"Where is it? Did you bring it with you?"

"My car was broken into, and it was taken, along with some old clothes. The officer that responded said he thought it was part of a rash of car break-ins."

She slumped back in her seat.

"I don't know if it would have been of any help anyway. As I said, the writing in it was illegible."

Cody looked as if she was thinking, then said, "Still, I would have liked to have had a look at it myself. Anything else taken from your car?"

"No. But I interrupted him while he was rifling through things. He might not have had a chance to take anything valuable." I decided not to mention what had happened during my brazen attempt to stop him. "I also talked to my neighbor, Audrey Cullen, and she thought the second car, the one that hit you, might have looked familiar to her."

Sunny sat up a bit straighter again. "Did she say where she thought she saw it before?"

"She stressed that she wasn't sure, but she thought she saw one of her son's friends drive one like it. She didn't say who the friend was, though."

Sunny jotted something down on the back of one of the papers by her laptop. "I'll ask them to have someone go by and talk to her again."

"It was kind of a non-descript car. She said she could be mistaken." I had trouble believing a kid could be involved in something like this, though I knew that was naive.

Sunny was quiet for a moment, then said, "True, it did look like a common car, and we don't have a make or model, but it would be very telling if we check the friend's car and it has a broken passenger side headlight or a dent in the fender." She motioned to her leg.

"Good point." That would be a good identifying feature, depending on how worried the driver was about being found. They could have gotten it fixed quickly. "Do you think that if you checked with local garages you might be able to find out if anyone brought in a light-colored car needing repair to the front passenger side?"

"Yes. I'll call around, but since we don't have much information on the vehicle, we would be throwing a wide net. Also, I've learned that not everyone is eager to share information with the police if it could get a friend or good customer in trouble."

Sunny picked up the pen and paper again. "So, how about you? Do you remember anything more about the car that hit me, or did you see anyone who was in the car?'

"No, I'm afraid I was so shocked to see it coming towards us at such a high rate of speed that I didn't notice much. My reflex was to get Bruno and myself out of its path."

She nodded, "Well, keep thinking about it. I just realized last evening that I saw another person in the front seat in addition to the driver. But I don't remember what either looked like, or even if they were male or female. I was a bit shocked myself when the car hit me."

"Understandable. How are you feeling today? Do you have much pain from your leg?"

She grimaced. "Still hurts, but the doc said it would for a while. The incision is starting to itch a little, but I've been taking my antibiotics, so I hope that is a good sign and that it's healing."

"I'll take a look and see what it looks like today." I had her scoot to the end of the sofa so I could get at her dressing. "It looks much better." I checked her head wound and decided her stitches could come out in a day or two.

I smiled at her as I put my dressing supplies back in my bag. "Everything looks great today. Glad to see you're 'doing what you are told,' as your daughter would say."

"Just as long as I can get back to normal soon. This doing what I'm told doesn't always work for me."

I didn't want to discourage her by pointing out it was going to be a long time before she was back to her "old" self, so I just said, "Healing takes time; sometimes you just have to give in and be patient." However, I knew her well enough now to know patience wasn't her strong suit.

As I prepared to leave, I said, "Maybe Audrey will be able to tell one of your colleagues more about the car."

Sunny went back to whatever she had pulled up on her laptop. "We'll see."

Chapter Eleven

I had an appointment to check on Kimberly Burke after her recent abdominal surgery. I finished checking her wound and we were discussing pain control when her cell phone rang. She looked at the screen and said, "I'm sorry, I need to get this."

As I waited for her to finish her call, I could hear her side of the conversation.

"What time will the soccer game end? Okay, but you'll have to wait for your father to pick you up, I'm still not supposed to drive." She looked to me for confirmation and I nodded. "I'll call him and let him know." She put the phone down and said, "My daughter. Her school's boys' soccer team is playing in the finals in their league. All the girls have a crush on one or another of the players, so there's no question that they 'really need to' stay after school and support the team." She rolled her eyes, "I remember those days."

I smiled, "When I was in high school it was the football team that drew the most adoring crowds. Which, of course, included me." I'd had a huge crush on one of the linebackers.

Audrey Cullen had made a big deal of how her son was one of the team's star players. I remembered what Charlie said about her probably holding something back. This was my opportunity to try to talk to her one more time about the car she told me looked familiar, and to see if she had really told the police all she saw that day. I decided I'd stop at the soccer field after my last appointment of the day.

"I have a friend whose son plays on the team. Maybe I'll stop by and see how they're doing. What time did she think the game would end?" I crossed my fingers behind my back as I stretched the truth to breaking.

"Leah said she needed to be picked up around five. Who's your friend's son?"

"Tyler Cullen."

Kimberly smirked. "Yes, I know who he is. The captain. I'm sure your friend is proud."

I wasn't sure what to make of her comment. "Do you know Audrey Cullen? You sound as if there is some tension there."

"Not really. We've met at school functions a few times. She's just very focused on her son, and she works hard to make sure everyone else is also." She grimaced as she shifted her position in her chair. "I'm sorry, that was not a kind thing to say. I hope I didn't offend you."

"No, of course not. I asked you about her." I was certainly getting a clearer picture of Audrey, and it reinforced my feelings that she would hesitate before giving the authorities any information that might taint her son's reputation.

I motioned for Kimberly to remain seated and left some supplies for her to change her own dressing, told her to call her doctor if she noticed any signs of infection, and said goodbye.

After I finished my last patient for the day, I rushed to the field to get there before the game ended and while the lot was still full.

I thought about what Sunny said about perhaps having noticed more that day than I initially remembered. If that light-colored car was in the lot at the soccer field, seeing it again could shake that memory loose. If nothing else, I could check for cars with recent damage.

I suddenly realized just how many light-colored sedans of various makes there actually were. Audrey said she thought the car she recognized belonged to a friend of her son. I had to admit that whoever the friend was, it was possible he didn't play on the team, or just wasn't at the game. When the police contacted her again to question her about what she saw, Audrey said she changed her mind and was not sure at all it resembled the car she had in mind. I thought I would give it one more try and see if she would talk to me about it. Then again, maybe she was so angry I'd mentioned what she saw to the police that she wouldn't talk to me at all.

I searched the bleachers for Audrey and found her seated in a second row at the end on the home team side. My plan was to get her to step away with me for a few minutes and talk about what happened.

"Hi, Audrey. How is the game going?"

She looked at me in surprise. "We're winning. By a lot."

"Which one is your son? Tyler, right?"

"Coach took him and a couple of the other key players out for now. It gives some of the kids on the bench a chance to play when we are crushing the other team. What are you doing here?"

"I was wondering if we could talk for a couple of minutes." I motioned her to an area back from the bleachers where there were no spectators.

She hesitated, but then followed me.

"I've been involved in the care of Detective Cody, the officer who was injured in that shooting incident we witnessed. She wondered if you might remember more about that day now that things are calming down."

I could see her tense up. She held her hands out in a stop motion, "Look, as I told the cops, I don't really remember much about that day to begin with, and I am not getting any new memories. I'd just as soon be left out of it from now on." She began to stalk back toward her seat on the bleachers, and I rushed to follow her.

"I just wondered…." I was cut off from finishing what I was going to say by the sound of screaming coming from a wooded area on the opposite side of the soccer field.

"Help! Somebody come quick!" A teenaged girl came running from the brush. "Help! Three of the guys. I think they might be dying!"

I yelled, "Call 911" to Audrey, and I took off at a run across the field, dodging a few of the players and heading toward where the girl was pointing. I saw a couple of other adults also headed in that direction. As I neared the wooded area, I could see that play had completely ceased on the field, the players frozen in place. When I reached her, the girl motioned to two forms sprawled on the ground next to a large rock. A third boy looked like he was trying to sit up, then turned and vomited onto the ground next to him.

I knelt next to the first figure I came to and saw one of the men who I thought might be the coach squat down next to the other. "I have this one; I know CPR," he shouted to me.

"What happened?" I asked the vomiting boy who was now in a wobbly sitting-up position shaking his head. There was no time to wait for an answer, though. I yelled to one of the adults who had come to help to stay with him and make sure he remained conscious, and I turned toward the boy on the ground by me. He was pale and beginning to get a blue tinge to his lips. As I watched, he took one shallow breath. "Hey! Hey, wake up! You okay?" I shook him. He didn't respond, so I felt for a pulse. It was slow but strong. I shook him again to try to get him to take another breath. He did not, so I began rescue breathing. After several breaths, he began to lose his dusky blue look, and I saw him take a shallow breath. I looked over to see the second boy's rescuer was giving him breaths also and was relieved to see that boy had started to come around.

I could hear the angry questions and panicked voices of more parents behind me, and the soothing voices of those trying to calm them. Suddenly, a woman rushed toward me as I bent over my boy, and I heard someone say, "Anna, Anna, let her help him!"

I looked up briefly to see a woman being held back away from where we were working on the boys. I guessed she must be the boy's mother. She had a look of horror on her face.

The crying girl was now being comforted by a woman who said, "She says she thinks they were doing drugs."

There was a sob from behind me, but the boy I was resuscitating stopped breathing again, so I checked to make sure he still had a pulse and went back to giving him breaths. All the while, I prayed that the first responders were on their way.

I took a brief break in my rescue breathing and spied a woman in a red jacket standing at the edge of the small crowd that had gathered. I yelled, "I'm a nurse. I need my bag. Blue Subaru Forrester parked in the back row; license plate starts with ADU. My bag is on the seat on the front passenger side." I handed her my keys.

I was relieved to see her hurry away. I knew I had at least two Narcan inhaler doses in the bag. I looked over to check that the third boy was still awake and breathing and that someone was sitting with him to keep an eye on him.

Just then, Audrey Cullen burst through the group that had managed to slip through those parents who were doing their best to herd most of the spectators and players away from the area. She ran to the semi-conscious boy. "Tyler! My God! What happened?" Her voice was panicked.

I was still busy doing rescue breathing but heard one of the other parents answer her.

"I think they were getting high on pills. Jenna! What were they taking?"

Audrey didn't give the girl a chance to answer. "No! Tyler wouldn't do drugs! Ty, what happened?" He mumbled a reply, but it was impossible for me to make out what he said.

Just then, the woman I sent for my work bag returned and set the bag down next to me. "The ambulance is on the way."

I pulled out the case that held my nasal Narcan and administered a dose to the boy I had been helping. The spray of medication up his left nostril should work very quickly, but to be sure, I gave him a few more breaths while the drug had time to work. He began to struggle but then took a huge gasp of air and started breathing on his own. He started to retch, so I turned him onto his side. I hoped the one dose would last long enough to keep him breathing until the paramedics arrived. I did have one more dose of Narcan if needed, but I prayed that wouldn't happen. The second rescuer seemed to be doing a good job of keeping the third boy breathing, even if he still seemed only semi-conscious.

"They're here! Over here!" I could hear several people shouting.

Two of the responders went to check on the boys, and I spoke to the third paramedic, telling him who I was and what I knew. "When I got here, two boys were unconscious, and one, Tyler Cullen, was just regaining consciousness." I glanced toward where Tyler was now lying on the ground unconscious, his mother standing aside as one of the responders administered a dose of Narcan to him. "I don't know the names of the other boys."

"Connor Booth and Nick Myers." The coach had come to stand beside me.

I nodded toward the coach, "We began rescue breathing, and as soon as someone retrieved my medical bag from the car, I was able to give this boy a dose of Narcan." I motioned to the boy I had resuscitated. I looked at my watch, "That was about five minutes ago now." While the drug works fast, it may only last for a short time, so I knew there was a possibility all three would need more than one dose before the effects of whatever they took were out of their system.

The police had also arrived, and two officers were speaking to the parents of the boys, though from what I overheard, none of them seemed to know what the boys took or where they got it. Audrey was crying and loudly protesting that her son would not have voluntarily taken drugs.

I saw the girl, Jenna, standing off to the side, speaking to a very agitated-looking man, who I assumed must be her father. "No! I just want to wait until I'm sure they are going to be all right!"

I approached her and introduced myself, then said, "Were you with the boys when they went off into the woods? Did you see what it was they were taking or who it was that gave it to them?"

She looked down, refusing to meet my eyes. "No, I don't know who had the pills. I saw them going toward the party spot in the woods, and I followed." She looked up but began to blush, "I kind of am going out with Connor." At this, I heard her father make a snorting noise.

"Anyway, I was going to see what they were doing, and you know, talk to him, but when I got there, they were acting weird and offered me one of whatever it was they were taking. I said no, but right away, they started passing out. I didn't know what to do!" She started to cry again, and her father put an arm around her.

"You did the right thing," I said, "you called for help."

Her father said, "They'll be okay now. We need to go." He led her away.

The three boys all appeared stable enough now and were being loaded into the ambulances. The parents were given the information about where they would be taken and to meet the ambulances there. My initial mission of finding out what Audrey knew about the vehicle that hit Detective Cody seemed even more important now since whoever was driving was likely involved in getting the drugs the kids were taking. Before I could talk to her, however, Audrey left to follow Tyler to the hospital.

As I was heading back toward my car, a woman approached me and said, "Thank heaven you were here! Those boys were dangerously close to not making it." I recognized her as the woman in the red jacket who had run to get my work bag from my car.

"Thank you for acting so fast when I asked you to get my bag."

"I was glad to help." She held out her hand, "I'm Beth Forbes, my son is on the soccer team also."

"Is he a friend of the boys who overdosed?"

She shook her head, "Not really. I mean, he knows them from school and being on the team, but they don't hang out together or anything." She looked back toward the wooded area I had just left. "Like I said, Luke doesn't hang with that crowd, but I have overheard him and his friends talking, and they keep mentioning how the new assistant coach has really gotten tight with Tyler Cullen and his friends."

"And you think the assistant coach may have had something to do with what happened here today?"

"I don't want to falsely accuse someone of something so serious, but I don't trust the guy. As far as I'm concerned, he's still just a kid himself. He's a student at Southern Connecticut University. He strikes me as someone who likes to party and likes it that some of the team really look up to him." She looked around as if to check that no one was listening in on our conversation. "When coach Randall announced he had asked a college-age kid to help him with the team, a group of us parents protested. We thought one of the fathers would be a better choice. Coach Randall said he felt the boys might respond better to a younger role model." She shook her head.

"What is the assistant coach's name? Was he here today? I don't know if I saw him."

As Beth said, it would be a serious accusation to bring against someone, but I could mention it to Sunny Cody and see if she had information on him.

"His name is Beck Chandler. I saw him earlier at the start of the game, but he didn't seem to be around when all the trouble began." Her phone dinged to signal a text, and after checking it, she said, "Well, nice meeting you. I have to go. My son is looking for me." She waved and headed toward the parking lot.

I had to get home also. Bruno would be wondering where his dinner was, and while I had my neighbor's daughter take him out after she came home from school, he would need to go out again soon.

Chapter Twelve

I felt drained when I got home. Bruno seemed to sense how I was feeling and was extra affectionate in his greeting. I took him out in the back yard to play fetch with his ball and let him sniff around the back fence and check all was still secure. I felt my mood lift a bit as we went back into the house. After I fed Bruno and fixed myself a quick dinner, I settled on the sofa, Bruno's head resting in my lap. I stroked his soft fur and took deep breaths to relax. I had just gotten to the point where my mind was drifting when my phone rang. I didn't recognize the number but answered anyway.

"Melanie? This is Audrey Cullen."

"Hi. How is Tyler? Is he still in the hospital?"

I could hear her clear her throat as if she had been crying. "He seems all right now, but they are keeping him overnight to observe him. I'm staying with him." I heard her voice catch, "I called to thank you. He could have...if you hadn't been there...." She took a long deep breath. "This isn't Tyler. He doesn't do drugs."

I let her statement go unchallenged. He obviously did do drugs, at least once anyway, and it could have been the last thing he did. "Did he say what happened, how he came to take those pills this afternoon?"

She spoke as if she was much more in control of her emotions now. "The police questioned him. He said Nick gave them to them. He said he thought they would just mellow him out a little; that coach wasn't going to put him back in the game so he thought he could chill out."

"Do you think it might have been Nick's car you recognized that day on Windy Reed Road?"

"I thought maybe it was, but Tyler said Nick doesn't have a car, that he doesn't even have his license yet. Sorry, I need to get back to my son. However, I can never thank you enough for helping Tyler." She ended the call.

I sat stroking Bruno again, this time thinking about the events of the previous week.

My reverie was interrupted by the ding of a text on my cell phone. I saw I had a missed text, also. I looked at the most recent one. *Are you home?* It was from Justin. I typed back *Yes* and waited for his reply. He called instead of texting.

"Hi. Where were you? I texted you before to see if you wanted to meet for a quick dinner after work today."

In the confusion of all that had been going on, I hadn't even noticed the earlier text. "Sorry. I stopped by a soccer game to see if I could talk to my neighbor about what happened last week. Her son was playing, and I wanted to see if she would tell me any more about the car she recognized." I could hear him make a muffled sound on the other end. "Anyway, it's a good thing I was there. Some of the boys overdosed on pills and needed to be resuscitated."

"It really was lucky for the boys you were there, but I'm worried about you getting mixed up in investigating something that could put you in danger. Shouldn't the police be the ones who are following up on the shooting and tracking down who is involved in distributing those pills?"

I tensed up at his words but fought letting my annoyance come through in my reply, "I understand you're concerned, but all I'm doing is asking some questions."

"And ending up in the way of a maniac in a car and someone getting shot! I don't understand why you feel you need to get involved in this!"

I was a little rattled at first by his anger and tried to respond in a calm manner. "I am already involved. I was there. I saw what happened... and...I don't know, I just feel like if I can help in some way, I should." We had been dating for a couple of months already, and I felt like he should have realized by now that I would feel that way.

"Besides, when we met, I was in the middle of being threatened and then held hostage by the people responsible for my ex-husband's murder. You were nothing but supportive then."

He was silent for a minute. "That was different. You had no choice but to be involved then. Now you need to just let the people whose responsibility it is to solve the crimes do their job. I'm sure Detective Cody can ask a fellow officer to follow up on any information they receive. You can be helpful in much safer ways."

"Is that a suggestion or an order? And what if I already feel I'm involved in investigating this crime too?" I didn't even try to keep the outrage out of my voice now. "Look, I can see that we aren't going to get anywhere with this discussion tonight. Let's talk about this when we have calmed down." We were both silent for a few seconds, then I took a deep breath and said, "Sorry I missed your text before."

"It's all right. After I sent it, I got an emergency call; a dog who ate a whole bag of chocolate bars her owner bought for Halloween. The dog will be fine now, but I would have had to back out of dinner anyway." He sounded much more in control now.

We chatted for a couple of minutes more before we said good night, but I couldn't help feeling a slight awkwardness as we ended our call. Our earlier argument still hung heavy in the air. I wasn't sure which bothered me more, the fact that we were in such disagreement over whether or not I was being careless to involve myself in Cody's case or that Justin felt he had the right to tell me what to do.

It had been a long day, and I was tired. Bruno had begun to doze off curled up next to my hip, and I was trying to work up the energy to get up and take my shower. I decided it wouldn't hurt to wait a few more minutes because, after all, I didn't want to disturb Bruno. I still felt upset about the disagreement with Justin. I did understand that he was just concerned for my safety, but I also felt that I was acting in a way that felt right to me.

A flood of unwelcome and guilt-ridden memories came back to me. When I was growing up, I was close to my cousin Kenny. When he was fifteen, he and my aunt and uncle moved away, and we grew apart. I heard talk that he was having some problems and had gotten into some trouble over the years, but I didn't see him again until I was a junior in college. He showed up unannounced at my dorm. His hair hadn't been washed in some time, he was walking with a shuffle, and his speech was slurred. I was shocked at his appearance but thought I could see some of the old Kenny in the look he gave me when I first came down to meet him. He asked how I was doing and said he was proud of me for going to college and wanting to become a nurse, but he cut to the chase quickly. He wanted money. He would, of course, pay me back "when he got back on his feet."

I didn't know how to react at first. I knew he was abusing either drugs or alcohol, or maybe both. We had learned all about the signs of addiction in class and the problems the addicts and their loved ones faced because of it. I realized that any money I gave him might just be used to feed his addiction. That is what I told myself anyway. Besides, I had very little money myself.

I struggled with what was the right thing to do, but in the end, I decided to do what was easiest and give him what he'd asked for. "Um. I can help you out a little, Ken. Where are you staying? Have you talked to your parents? Maybe you should…."

The look in his eyes hardened. "If you have a couple of bucks to spare, I 'd appreciate it. But just skip the lectures, okay?"

I gave him all I had saved from my on-campus job for a trip I'd planned to take on spring break. He nodded his thanks, then shuffled away. A year later, I attended his funeral. Everyone said it was such a shame, that it was too bad he never got help with his problem, but that no one could help him until he wanted to help himself. While I knew there was some truth in that, deep in my heart, I felt I should have done something more. I felt shame and guilt that I hadn't tried harder to help.

It didn't take a degree in psychology to see that there probably was a connection between my experience with my cousin and how I reacted to situations today. In fact, Justin did have a degree in psychology, so I wondered why it was so difficult for him to see where I was coming from. But then, while we had shared certain intimacies, we hadn't gotten to the stage of our relationship where we aired out all our dark corners.

Bruno shifted from his position, snuggled against me, stretched, and yawned, causing me to stretch and yawn myself. "I agree, little buddy; time for bed."

Chapter Thirteen

The next morning after Bruno and I went out for our morning run, I called Sunny Cody to let her know what had happened at the soccer game the previous day and what Beth Forbes had told me about the assistant coach. I left a message when the call went to her voicemail. I wondered why she hadn't answered, but then I remembered she had an early appointment with Dr. Hackett for a follow-up. I asked her to let me know that she had gotten my message and if she had any questions.

By the end of the day, I hadn't heard back from Detective Cody, but I was sure she would have gotten someone to follow up on any information the police had on Beck Chandler. It could be that what Beth Forbes told me was just a case of a parent not being pleased with the coach's choice of assistant, but I'd felt it worth mentioning to Sunny Cody anyway.

I'd also not heard from Justin. I reasoned that he'd had a full schedule also. I decided to wait before I called him. I convinced myself it was not because I was being stubborn and waiting to see if he called me first. We'd ended our call on a pleasant note last night. At least superficially.

After I fed Bruno, I had my own dinner. As I ate, I kept checking my phone to see if I'd somehow missed a call. I finally had to admit I was being ridiculous in not just calling Justin. But somehow, I couldn't bring myself to make the first move. Not yet anyway.

The days were getting shorter, and I wanted to take Bruno for a quick walk before the sun set. I grabbed his leash, and he scampered over to me. I decided to just stick to walking on our road rather than taking a turn to walk on Windy Reed Road where it would be a bit too deserted at this hour. I still felt unsettled by the thought that someone had been watching me when we were there earlier in the week. When we came back toward our house, Bruno's tail suddenly started its happy wag, and he began to pull a bit on his leash. Lynn's car was in my driveway.

As she got out of her car, she said, "I thought I'd stop and say hello on my way home from giving my art lesson at the rec center." Lynn stooped to give Bruno a good ear scratching, then gave me a quick hug, "How are things?"

Just then, I noticed a car slowing in front of my house, then taking off quickly, spraying gravel from the side of the road.

Lynn spun around as the car sped down the road. "Yikes! What was that about?"

My road is not a main thoroughfare, and I didn't recognize the car as belonging to one of my neighbors. I did notice that it was a light gray sedan. "I don't know." A feeling like a slight electric charge ran through me, "Come on, let's go in. I'll make us tea."

Bruno went to rest on the floor under the kitchen table between both of us as we settled in with our tea.

Lynn gave me a brief update on what was going on at High Life Dermatology. There seemed to always be some drama, though nothing as earth-shaking as Artie's murder and the revelation of his illegal activities had been.

In any case, I was only half listening. I kept thinking about the light-colored car that hit Sunny. Maybe it was just a coincidence this car had passed my house. Maybe it had merely slowed to avoid hitting a squirrel or something. I was sure the car that had just passed had a rear bumper sticker. Was that an identifying feature we all may have missed on the car that hit Sunny?

"Anyway, I am trying to stay neutral in the whole disagreement," Lynn said.

I totally missed the story she had been telling me. "I'm sorry. I guess I didn't get all of that. What happened?"

"Never mind. It's silly anyway," Lynn said. "Are you alright? You seem a bit distracted. How are things going with you and Justin?"

"He still isn't thrilled with me helping Sunny Cody. But I'm sure we'll work it out." I gave her what I hoped was a reassuring smile. "What about you and

Alex? Are you still keeping your relationship a secret at the office?"

Her whole face lit up. "No. Of course, we keep it totally professional while we are at work, but somehow it got out that we are dating. Neither of us denies it now, and it doesn't seem to have affected my working relationship with the rest of the staff. Though, I do think Britany has a crush on Alex and wasn't too happy to find out he was taken."

"So, you working there part-time is no problem?"

She shook her head, "No. As a matter of fact, they offered me full-time since one of the other receptionists is leaving after she has her baby. I said no, though. The painting classes are working out well, and I've even increased the number of classes I'm giving."

"Have you told Alex about that guy who seemed to be stalking you? Have you shown him the note you got?"

"I didn't show him the note, but yes, I finally told Alex. He said if I notice him following me or lurking around my condo again, to call him. I haven't noticed the guy lately, however. But then, I haven't been home as much either." She smiled again, "What with work, my classes, and…uhm… spending a lot of time at Alex's."

"That's great! So, things really are going well between the two of you, then?"

"Yes. We found a connection quickly. As it turns out, we both have similar histories. Married young and then divorced when it turned out our partners were unfaithful. His was a much messier divorce than mine and Artie's and certainly more dramatic than mine and Doug's. Anyway, maybe for me third time's a charm!"

I winced at the unfaithful part, though I had no idea Artie was still married when I met him. "Wow! It's looking like it's that serious?"

She nodded, "I think so. As far as I'm concerned, it is."

I was happy for her, and I hoped she was right about this relationship lasting. Even though I was a little worried. It all seemed to happen very quickly. They had only started dating three months ago. "That's great. I'll be waiting for the official announcement."

She laughed and crossed her fingers, "Well, I don't know. I hope I'm not getting ahead of myself, but it feels right."

Bruno hopped up then and ran over to the kitchen door, letting out a short "woof!" signaling his need to go out.

Lynn got up and put her cup in the sink. "I'll let you tend to Bruno. I need to go anyway."

"Oh, to see Alex?"

She laughed, "No, I'm going back to my condo tonight. I'll let myself out." She bent down to pet Bruno again and planted a kiss on top of his head before she left.

It was full dark by now, so I grabbed a sweatshirt and my flashlight as I went out into the backyard with Bruno.

He quickly did his business, but then perked his ears and ran toward the back fence. Then he jumped back and started to bark frantically. It is a tall stockade fence, and I couldn't see over it, but I shone my flashlight along it anyway. I couldn't see anything, and Bruno settled down with a final growl to warn whatever it was to stay away.

It was probably a raccoon, or maybe some deer foraging through the brush on the other side of the fence, I reasoned. But then I remembered the black-clad figure ransacking my car, and I hustled back into the house with Bruno.

I thought about the car I'd seen earlier. Why would the person who hit Sunny be interested in me, and how would they know where I lived? How would they even know I was looking for them? Unless someone told them. The only people who knew, besides Sunny, were Lynn, Justin, Charlie Duggan, and Audrey Cullen.

I jumped when my phone dinged that I'd gotten a text. Not Justin. A reminder of my dentist's appointment on Tuesday.

Chapter Fourteen

The following day I had an appointment in the mid-morning with Sunny Cody. It was scheduled to be my last official visit on behalf of Coretrack since her wound was almost healed. She would, of course, still need to continue her physical therapy. According to Tim Thorpe, her physical therapist, she was doing well with that also, if pushing herself a bit faster than recommended to get back the function of her right knee.

I was about to ring the bell at Sunny's front door when it opened, and a man rushed out, nearly knocking me over.

He grabbed my arms to steady me and said, "Oh! Sorry. I didn't know you were there." He paused a moment, studying my face as if he knew me, but then let go and turned to go down the front steps.

I realized he looked familiar to me, also. I turned around to watch him head toward the dark sedan parked across the street from the house. I heard Sunny's voice behind me.

"Jerk!" She stood balanced on her crutches, also watching him head to his car. "Sorry. Come on in, Melanie."

As I entered, I asked, "Who was your visitor? You didn't seem very happy with him."

She just glared at the place where his car had been parked and said, "A colleague of mine, but someone I could totally have done without seeing today." She shoved the front door closed behind me.

I could smell the delicious scent of tomato sauce wafting from the direction of the kitchen. "Smells like you are up to managing yourself in the kitchen now, too."

She laughed and motioned for me to put my things down and take a seat. "No. I have convinced my mother I don't need twenty-four-hour care anymore, but she still insists on stopping over most days to cook for Katie and me." She settled herself onto the sofa, her crutches propped beside her. "I wouldn't think of arguing with her about that!"

I noticed she had a lot of papers spread out on the coffee table in front of her, and some of them looked like the ones I'd seen before.

I was about to mention them and ask if she knew if anyone had spoken to Beck Chandler about what happened at the soccer game when her mother, Pauline Moran, popped her head into the room. "I'm going to pick up Katie at pre-K. Don't give Miss Bass a hard time." She winked at me.

As her mother left, Sunny wiggled forward a bit and pulled up the cut-off right leg of her sweatpants so I could look at her incision. "What do you think?"

I removed the dressing and the knee brace to inspect Sunny's wound. "This looks great. I don't think it needs to be covered anymore. Is it still painful?"

"It aches a little after PT. But nothing terrible. Nothing I need to take a pain med for."

I would bet most people would describe the pain as more than aching a little, but if she was not hampered from doing her physical therapy by discomfort, then it was fine.

"You know this is the last visit I'll have to do related to your injuries from the accident," I said as I began to pack up my supplies. "I was wondering if you know if anyone has interviewed the assistant soccer coach to see if he is connected to what happened the other evening. Also, were the investigators able to find out where Nick Meyers got the drugs?"

She was quiet for a moment, her jaw tightening, then she said, "That guy who was leaving when you got here was Greg Langley. He's in charge now of the investigation into the event on Windy Reed Road and how it's connected to the whole drug operation."

"You don't seem very happy with that decision."

"He's a lazy fool. He said there was no evidence to suspect this Chandler of involvement in supplying drugs to those kids. That it could have been any number of people, and that it wasn't 'worth ruining the reputation of the guy just because a parent is upset she couldn't get her own way.'" Her look now mirrored the look she had given Officer Langley. "As for Nick Meyers, he says he 'found' the pills in the boy's bathroom at school. He's sticking to that story, and Langley says he believes him. Langley says he's working on finding whoever left the pills there." She made a sound somewhere between a grunt and a growl.

I suddenly remembered where I'd seen him before. He had responded to the 911 call after the shooting and Sunny being hit by the car. "Wasn't Detective Langley one of the officers on the team, set to back you up after the drug exchange? I remember seeing him that day."

She grunted again, "Yes. Not that he would have been my choice, but he had already been made part of the team. He suggested I could help them out. I thought he was going to dump most of the work on me and claim all the glory when we apprehended the dealers that day. I would have declined his offer, but I got the word that Darren Bourne had some information for me."

"About your husband's murder." I motioned to the papers on the coffee table.

She nodded, "That's what I thought. I was going to question him once we took him into custody. He had already made a deal for supplying the location of the drug distribution. I was surprised when I was assigned to just confirm the deal was about to go down and then give the team the okay to move in. My plan was to take charge of Darren Bourne and talk to him before we got him back to the station."

"Things didn't work out that way, though," I said.

"No."

I motioned again to the papers spread out in front of her. "Were you able to find anything in those to help you?"

She sighed and leaned forward, splaying the papers further apart with her fingers. "Not really. I have been over the report a hundred times, but nothing new pops out at me. That's one reason I was so aggravated with Langley. He wrote the original report. I told him I thought there was more to the story than what it looked like at first. I asked him to dig a little, see if anyone knew who had given Brian the tip about the robbery and why he responded alone the night he was shot. I know Langley is not one to rock the boat, he's too lazy to stir up trouble, but he was a friend of Brian's. All I'm asking him to do is talk to a few people again, see if anybody has any answers."

"Will he do it?"

"He said I had to let it go. We all miss Brian, but he was killed in the line of duty by one of the bad people, and that bad guy got killed by another bad guy. When I got angry at what he said, he agreed to ask around a little. He won't."

I checked my watch. I had another appointment scheduled in twenty minutes. "I have to leave. But I have a feeling you think someone should talk to Beck Chandler and see if he knows anything about the drugs the boys took the other day. I suppose I could find a way to talk to him. If you want me to."

She looked relieved, "Just see what he says, and get back to me to let me know what you find out."

I felt a small knot in my stomach thinking about what Justin might say when he found out I was getting more involved in the case. I was going to have to resolve the issue with him if we were going to continue to have a relationship. But that also made me think of his grandfather. Charlie might have heard something while monitoring his police radio, might recognize the name, or at least might have some useful thoughts on the young man. And I was going to have to tell Charlie that I think he was wrong, that we couldn't keep the fact that he was helping me from Justin.

Chapter Fifteen

I realized it was ridiculous to keep waiting for Justin to call, so I decided I would check in with him at lunch time. When I took out my cell phone to make the call, I saw he had already tried to call me. The message he left asked if we could meet at my house after work. I texted back that that would be fine and ended with a heart emoji.

Ida Wilkes was my last patient of the day, and she lived only a half mile from Charlie Duggan. I had some time until I was to meet Justin at my house, so I decided to stop in and see Charlie. I thought I better warn him that I planned to tell Justin that we were doing a little investigating on behalf of Sunny Cody. Also, I planned to ask him if he knew anything or could find out anything about Beck Chandler.

This time Charlie just called, "Come on in." When I knocked at his door. When I entered, he was seated in his chair and had his prosthetic leg on.

"Wow, that's not like you to invite just anybody to come in. Are you feeling all right?" I said.

"I'm just fine. Saw your car turn in." He motioned to the window opposite where he sat.

He pushed aside the newspaper he was reading and said, "Well, what's the story behind what happened the other day at the soccer field? I heard the call on my scanner. Saved the day, did ya?"

"I went to the game to see if my neighbor could tell me any more about who could have been driving the car that hit Detective Cody. I didn't expect to have to deal with a crisis when I got there." I told him what had happened after I spoke to Audrey Cullen, and who the boys were, and that Nick was the one who "found" the pills and gave them to the other boys.

He grunted, then said, "Found them, huh? Police going to go back and see if the boy changes his story with a little encouragement?"

"Sunny Cody says the officer in charge is satisfied that Nick is telling the truth. It is possible, but..."

"Not likely. Sounds like the boy doesn't want to get somebody else in trouble," he said.

"I did talk to one parent who says she has suspicions about the new assistant coach, Beck Chandler. She doesn't have any proof or anything, just that he is still a student himself at Southern, and something about him made her not want to trust him. She said he's become close to several boys on the team, including the boys who overdosed. Have you ever heard anything about him?"

Charlie shook his head, "Can't say I have."

"The police don't think they have enough reason to question him, but Detective Cody thinks it wouldn't hurt to follow up on the parent's suspicions. I told her I'd talk to him."

"You say he's a student at the college? I could maybe contact a fella I used to know who works campus security. I could see if he knows the kid and what he thinks of him. I'll let you know what I find out." He scribbled something on a scrap of paper he grabbed from the coffee table in front of him.

"Thanks, Charlie." I hesitated a moment, then said, "You mentioned once that you didn't think we should tell Justin you were helping me. Why did you say that?"

He looked away from me for a moment, then said, "I imagine he isn't too thrilled with you getting involved with this Cody's investigation, is he?"

"That's putting it mildly. He seems really upset by it. All I'm doing is asking some questions. I don't think I'm putting myself in danger. His anger seems out of proportion to what I'm doing. Besides, now that I got involved with those boys who nearly died from taking those drugs, I feel a responsibility to do whatever I can to help find who is distributing them."

"I can't say I blame you, but Justin's had a bad experience with someone he cared about putting themselves in a dangerous situation. Not my story to tell, but let's just say he cares a lot about you and doesn't want a repeat of what happened before." Charlie leaned back in his chair, "I wasn't ready yet to put my head on the chopping block, cause I know he'll have a few words for me." He winked at me. "I guess you need to tell him now. As for me, I'll say I was just trying to keep an eye on you, keep you from getting in too much trouble."

"Are you?"

"Well, if I need to, but I think you can take care of yourself from what I see. I just want to keep a hand in solving crimes, even if I have to do it from my chair. I'll ask the guy I know about Chandler and get back to you."

I checked the time and saw I better hurry to get home before Justin got there. "I need to leave; I'm meeting Justin this evening, and we are going to 'have a talk.'"

Charlie reached over and patted my hand. "Good luck. Don't let my pig-headed grandson give you a hard time."

That made me pause for a minute. What if Justin and I couldn't work out our differences? I felt my stomach clench.

Charlie must have read the distress on my face because he said, "Don't worry, my grandson may be stubborn, but he isn't stupid. He'll see the light. Eventually."

I let myself out, telling Charlie I'd let him know if I found out anything when I talked to Beck Chandler. Right now, I was curious to hear the incident Charlie had alluded to that caused Justin to be so adamant I stay out of Cody's investigation. I felt a little chagrined that I had just assumed it was him being controlling.

I was able to get home, feed Bruno, and let him out to do his business before Justin arrived.

Forty-five minutes later, when I heard Justin's car pull into the driveway, I felt a bolt of apprehension. I wasn't sure how to make him understand my need to be involved in the police investigation of Sunny's hit and run, and how that led to the wider investigation of drug abuse in our community. More importantly, I didn't understand why I needed to explain myself.

However, just in case, I had two responses ready to go depending on what he said. The first was a gracious and warm acceptance of his support if he had come to the realization that my curiosity and desire to help were part of who I was. The second, in case he still objected to my actions, a firm statement that I could recognize when I was getting myself in a situation I was not equipped to handle. I did realize that I had indeed gotten in a bit over my head in the past, but I had learned from that experience, and now I knew when I needed to call for backup before plunging ahead.

I opened the door to let Justin in. Bruno was dancing around my ankles, for once not picking up on my feelings in his joy to see Justin. As he passed me, Justin gave me a quick peck on the cheek. His less-than-enthusiastic greeting made me think he was also unsure how to address the issue that had come between us.

After he came in, he stooped down to pet Bruno and murmur a greeting and a "good boy!" to him, but afterward, rather than taking a seat, he just stood in the living room looking everywhere but at me. Then he said, "Melanie…."

I blurted, "Coffee or tea?" before he could finish what he had started to say. I realized I was stalling, but I always felt better with something hot to drink in front of me before confronting a difficult situation.

"Coffee. I'll get it down for you." I kept the coffee on a top shelf, since I usually drink tea, and Justin had gotten into the habit of reaching it for me.

I bustled around the kitchen, boiling the water for tea, brewing coffee, and putting two pumpkin chocolate chip muffins I had made on a plate. Justin sat at the table. Bruno jumped up to put his front paws on Justin's knees, and Justin was murmuring to him and scratching his ears. I felt a little catch in my chest as I remembered the first time Justin and I met. I had gone to see him in hopes of him helping Bruno overcome the PTSD he suffered after Artie's death. As I watched, though, now it looked more like Justin was trying to calm himself rather than Bruno.

I sat opposite Justin and took a sip of my tea and placed a muffin on my plate. Despite how tense I felt, I was starving. I noticed Justin didn't touch his coffee or help himself to a muffin, however. He cleared his throat and said, "Melanie, I've been thinking, and I realize that you feel you have to get involved when you think you can help someone."

I tried to read his expression, thinking I could get my "thank you for your understanding" speech ready, but then he took a deep breath and continued.

"However, I'm not comfortable with you constantly putting yourself in danger. I realize we have only been seeing each other for a few months, but I have come to care very deeply about you, and I don't think I can deal with the constant fear of something happening to you."

I started to reach for his hand across the table to assure him I cared deeply for him also. He inched his hand away, and I noticed he had become pale.

The look he gave me then was one that I thought he must give a pet before he euthanized them. He said, "So if you feel you have to continue to be involved in this investigation, I think it's probably better if we take a break from seeing each other."

I hadn't expected that. I hoped my jaw hadn't literally dropped. I quickly went from shock to anger. No discussion, no chance to use response number two, where I told him I was older and wiser now and could decide when I needed to step back from a potential danger. No input into whether *I* thought we should stop seeing each other. Sometime during the last few disastrous minutes, Bruno had come to snuggle against my feet under the table. He really did know how to read a situation, I guess.

"That's it? I have no say in what happens with us?"

"You know how I feel about you playing detective. And you clearly don't plan to stop, so I guess that's your answer. I cannot go through..." He stopped what he was saying and leapt up out of his chair, causing it to rattle against the table and startle Bruno. The dog jumped up and let out two frightened barks.

I picked up Bruno to calm him, though I was sure he could tell I was not very calm myself. "Go through what?"

He was quiet for a moment. I couldn't tell whether it was to calm himself or to decide if he was going to answer my question. He ran a hand through his hair, causing it to stand up in front, and under other circumstances, I might have laughed at how he looked.

"Let's just say this isn't the first time I've had to worry about something happening to someone that is close to me."

It wasn't lost on me that neither of us had used the "L" word in describing our feelings for each other. I know I was certainly confused about how I felt about him at this minute.

"Maybe we can work this out if you tell me exactly what happened to make you feel this way. Your grandfather mentioned you had a bad experience, but …."

Justin looked thunderstruck. "You were talking to my grandfather about this?"

"He said I'd have to ask you, but…"

"Is he involved in what you are doing too? Never mind, I'm sure he is. That's why he wanted to talk to you, isn't it?" He was pacing now. "Stubborn, meddling old man! And now he's encouraging you to stay involved in this whole crime thing!"

"I can think for myself and make my own decisions. Charlie is only offering to be a sounding board for my ideas and giving me his own take on the situation! What he and I talk about is none of your business anyway."

Justin nodded, "You're right. It is no longer any of my business."

It looked like Justin was getting hold of his emotions again, but mine were coming to a boil. "If he's stubborn, then you certainly inherited the trait!"

Justin didn't respond, but took his untouched coffee cup, dumped the coffee in the sink, turned, and headed to the door.

I followed him, trying to think of another wounding comment to make because the full meaning of what he said had begun to sink in. He had broken up with me. After he left, I collapsed onto the sofa. I had not wanted it to end this way. I had not wanted it to end at all. I was so sure we could work things out. Bruno crawled into my lap, licking my chin as the tears dripped from it. I had another awful thought—did this mean that now I had to find another veterinarian for Bruno?

Chapter Sixteen

The next day I woke up feeling groggy. After what had proved to be an emotionally draining evening, I hadn't slept well. It was a sunny day and the temperature was in the mid-fifties, so I decided a run along the path at Hammonasset Beach State Park might be just the thing to clear my head. Besides, Bruno loved it when I jogged along that path. The breezes at the beach were cooler than those at my house, so I grabbed a sweatshirt, put Bruno in the car, and I set off.

My plan for dealing with the breakup with Justin was to avoid thinking about it. I couldn't totally banish my feelings of sorrow, hurt, and anger, but as I jogged along, I tried to focus on work, and what I could do to help Sunny Cody with the investigation. I felt I had a personal stake in helping find out who was putting so many lives in danger now. I'd been witness to the killing of one man, the injury of a police officer, and involved in saving the lives of three young men. All seemed to be connected to the same narcotics ring.

I thought the best chance for me to talk to Beck Chandler was after a game. After I finished work for the day, I called Audrey Cullen to see when the next soccer game was scheduled.

"Hi Audrey, it's Melanie. I was wondering how Tyler is doing. No more ill effects from the other day, I hope."

"He's doing fine, thank heavens. Not happy that he's grounded for the rest of the month, but we keep reminding him he could have ended up in a lot worse circumstances."

"Well, I'm glad he is all right now. He must be sad not to be able to play with the team on Thursday, though." I took a chance on when I thought the next game might be.

She hesitated a minute, then said, "The next game is tomorrow. After some discussion among the parents, Coach Randall, and with the school board it was decided to let Tyler and the other boys play. They are really close to making the playoffs. Tyler, Nick, and Collin are three of their best players. I think they learned their lesson with what happened to them after trying those pills on Friday. I don't think they'll make the same stupid choice again." She chuckled, "Besides, Coach told them they are only allowed to be on the field playing or have their butts on the team bench. If they even need to use the rest room a parent or assistant Coach Chandler has to accompany them."

I wasn't a parent, but I felt stunned that such a serious incident seemed to have been glossed over without major repercussions. However, my ears perked up at the mention of Beck Chandler's name. "Oh, I didn't notice the assistant coach at the game the other day. Was he there?"

"I saw him talking to the boys, getting them pumped up before the game, but I didn't notice if he was there or not afterward. But then, I was more focused on what was happening with Tyler."

"Of course," I said. "If the assistant coach is half as good as Coach Randall, it is no wonder the boys are so motivated on the field." I didn't really know anything about Coach Randall except he was well-trained in CPR and that the team and parents seemed to love him.

"You said his assistant's name is Beck? Has he been working with Coach Randall long? What do you think of him?"

"Beck Chandler is young, but Tyler says he's a good guy. Evidently, he was a star player on his high school and college soccer teams until he got injured." Her voice changed in pitch, "Why do you ask?"

I tried to think of a quick lie, but the truth would probably get me more information. "One of the parents told me after everything that happened the other day that she was concerned about his youth, that he might be trying to be more of a buddy to the kids than was wise."

"Humph! Let me guess. Beth Forbes, right? She's been raising a stink about Beck Chandler being hired as a coach ever since her husband was turned down for the job. Tyler really looks up to Beck, and he's excellent at getting the best performance out of the boys on the team. I don't know why Beth even approached you with her complaints. Just ignore her and her ugly suspicions."

"Well, I'm glad Tyler is back to himself, and tell him good luck in tomorrow's game." I still had every intention of speaking to Beck after the game, but now I began to wonder if there wasn't an element of revenge in what Beth Forbes told me. One thing that Audrey said did stick in my mind though: Beck had suffered a career-ending injury. I wondered how severe it was and if he had required heavy-duty pain meds during his recovery.

The next day I arrived at the soccer field just as the game was ending. I stayed in my car and watched as the players left the field. I hoped to avoid Audrey Cullen as it would be hard to explain my presence at a game again. I saw Tyler walking off the field with a young man who looked to be just a bit older than he was. They exchanged a high- five and then Tyler walked over to where his mother was talking to three of the other mothers. I saw the young man he had been speaking to walk back toward the field. I noticed he had a slight limp, so I assumed that was Beck Chandler.

He was gathering soccer balls and placing them in a net bag when I approached him. "Hi, Coach Chandler, good game today." I sincerely hoped it had been.

He turned to me and gave me a polite smile. "Yes, the guys are totally stepping up their game. They really want the championship."

"I'm so glad they were able to put that awful incident that happened the other day behind them." I saw a quick look of confusion wash over his face, followed by a look of comprehension.

"Yeah, that could have been tragic, huh? I'm glad it turned out okay."

"It was very frightening." I held back on mentioning my own part in the resuscitation. "Luckily, Coach Randall knew what to do. It was chaotic, so I'm sorry, but I don't remember if you were there also."

He finished gathering all the soccer balls and cinched the bag closed. "No, I had...an appointment."

"I just wondered, because a lot of the parents were wondering just how the boys got hold of the drugs they took. Since you are so close to some of the team members and being of college age, there was some thought that maybe you...."

"Whoa! I have no idea how they got whatever they took!" He picked up the bag of equipment and then slammed it down. "I know what some of those biddies are saying about me and that they didn't want coach making me his assistant, but I'm not getting blamed for what happened to those kids the other day!"

I had obviously touched a nerve with my question. "I was just going to say that maybe you might have overheard something from one of the boys or maybe have some suspicions of your own about what is going on."

He looked at me as if he was just then really seeing me. "I'm sorry. Whose mother did you say you were?"

I was searching my mind for a plausible response but was saved from answering. He saw something over my shoulder that caused him to grab the equipment and say, "Sorry. I have to go." He began to rush away, his limp seeming a bit more pronounced.

I turned around to see Detective Langley crossing the field toward us. It looked like Detective Cody was wrong about Langley; he must have decided there was a reason to question Chandler after all. The young man started to veer away from Langley, but I heard the detective call out to him, and Chandler stopped. I walked slowly toward my car, watching what happened when Langley caught up with him. I veered over to walk as close as possible to where they were speaking without being obvious about it. Whatever questions Langley had for Chandler, he was asking them right there rather than taking him someplace to interrogate him. I kept my eyes forward and looked down just in case Detective Langley remembered where he had seen me before. As I got closer, the only thing I could hear, however, was Chandler saying loudly, "I told you, no! I don't..." then he dropped his voice again.

I glanced at the pair as I passed and saw Langley staring intently at Chandler as if assessing whether he believed what he had told him or not. Detective Langley looked like he was about to say something, but then saw me and stopped.

I waved at him as if we were well acquainted and rushed to my car. I had a feeling Detective Cody would not want me to let her colleague know she sent me on an investigative mission. I'd let her know that Beck Chandler denied supplying drugs to the boys on the team, as would be expected. However, judging by the way he reacted when he saw Detective Langley, he knew something that he wasn't eager to share. I'd ask Detective Cody if Langley had any better luck getting the information out of him.

Chapter Seventeen

I wondered if Charlie had had a chance to talk to his friend yet. I decided to give him a call that evening and find out. Also, I was anxious to see if Justin had paid him a visit and, if so, how it went.

He was no more prompt answering his phone than he was known to be answering the door. I was about to hang up and try again when I heard a gruff "Yeah?" in my ear.

"Hi Charlie, sorry to bother you; it's Melanie."

"It's me who's sorry. Sorry my grandson is such a fool. Guess I was wrong about how bright he is since he doesn't know when he should hang onto someone."

"He told you how things went then. I'm afraid during our quarrel I mentioned you were helping me. I hope he wasn't too hard on you." I didn't really think Charlie would take much lecturing from Justin, but I would feel bad about being the cause of a rift between the two of them.

"Oh, he had a few things to say, but I set him straight, gave him a bit to think about, too." I heard a grunt, then a soft thud that made me think he'd taken off his prosthetic lower leg again. "I talked to my friend. Seems that Chandler fella was in a bit of trouble before. Word was that he had a history of minor infractions as a juvenile, and last semester nearly got himself kicked out of school and is on probation now."

"Do you know what happened?"

"Larry said it had something to do with a load of illegal substances that were found in his possession. He said the kid was gone from school for about a week, but then suddenly he was back. Larry heard the family made a big stink about him being framed by someone, and then all of a sudden, the evidence disappeared. One of the two security guards who found the stash was suspected of getting rid of the evidence. The cops couldn't prove it, but the guy was fired by the school anyway. My friend thinks it was somebody else that dumped the drugs but doesn't know who. In any case, he heard the charges against the Chandler kid were dropped."

"And the high school hired him as an assistant coach? I'm surprised."

"I guess he used to be some big deal soccer player, and the coach there at the high school vouched for him. He said since he was never convicted, he shouldn't be punished. I always found the old 'where there's smoke, there's fire' theory to be true. If it was me, I wouldn't be so sure he's innocent."

"Given his history, then it's no wonder he seemed so nervous when Detective Langley arrived." I told Charlie what had happened when I spoke to Beck Chandler and that he had denied having anything to do with giving the drugs to the boys on the team. "His past problems also could explain why he was so defensive when I first brought up the subject."

"What does your detective friend have to say about what the kid told you?"

"I haven't spoken to her yet. I plan on stopping over there after my scheduled appointments tomorrow. I'll let her know what we found out."

"Might be she already knows about the trouble this Chandler was in before, or at least can find out from the official records. Anyway, I told my friend you would keep his name out of it when you mentioned it to Cody."

I didn't point out that he hadn't told me the man's full name. "Okay, I won't say where I learned about it. Like you said, she might be able to get more information herself by calling someone who was involved in the investigation." I had one more thing I wanted to say before I hung up, however, and I took a second to decide how I wanted to say it. "Um, Charlie, about Justin.... I appreciate you trying to make him see reason regarding our relationship, but he and I should be the ones to decide if there is any more to be said and if we can get over this."

I heard a loud "Phsst!" On the other end. "I have my own opinion, but last time I looked, there wasn't a councilor's certificate hanging on my wall. I said what I think, and I know enough to keep out of the middle of this."

"Thank you. Now I better let you go. Also thank you for checking with your friend about Beck Chandler."

"Be sure and let me know if you find out anything more, or if you got anything else I can look into for you." He hung up.

It was late, and I realized my lack of sleep over the past two nights was catching up with me. Bruno let out a yawn and looked at me like he also knew it was bedtime. After I took him out one last time, we settled into bed. The last thing I remember was him snuggling to get comfortable against my hip. I was out as soon as my head hit the pillow.

Chapter Eighteen

I had the day off, and my plan was to catch up on housework and laundry, take Bruno for a long walk, and then swing by Sunny Cody's. I'd tell her how my questioning Beck Chandler went and let her know what Charlie found out. I also wanted to know if she talked to Detective Langley about what he'd learned from Chandler.

I had gotten the house back into decent shape and was putting away my clean laundry when my cell phone rang. I looked at the display before answering: Lynn.

I could tell she was brimming with excitement as soon as I answered.

"Melanie, guess what! Alex is taking me out to dinner at Prime tonight, and I heard him talking to someone about a 'special' package he wanted to be sure was all set for him to pick up. I think this might be it, that he plans to ask me to marry him!"

"Wow! Congratulations!" I truly did feel happy for her, but I fought to prevent myself from adding, "Are you sure this is a good idea since you haven't been together that long? You both have a history with failed marriages, do you think you *really* know him?" I realized my own recent breakup had left a bitter taste in my mouth as far as love was concerned.

She continued on a more cautious note, "Well, I don't know for sure, but he has been dropping some hints about something big coming up." I heard her take a deep breath, then say, "I know I sound like a love-struck teenager, but since I moved to Connecticut, I feel like I really am able to start a whole new life. When I met Alex, I just knew he was the right person for me at this time in my life."

Well, who can squash such joy and optimism, I thought. "I'm so glad things are working out for you. You deserve to be genuinely happy." I was still amazed that even though Lynn and I had both been married to the same man, instead of being jealous of and disliking each other, we had developed a true friendship.

"Thanks, Mel. I'll let you know if my suspicions were right. I better get back to work now. Talk to you later."

Lynn hadn't asked about how things were going with Justin, and I certainly wasn't going to bring her mood down by telling her. I took a few minutes to feel sorry for myself, but as Bruno hopped up and sat beside me, I petted him and realized how silly I was being. Obviously, Justin and I weren't as compatible as I had thought, and better to find out now before things got even more serious.

Clouds had started to move in, and the temperature was dropping, so instead of walking, I took Bruno out in the back yard to run off some energy before the rain started. After I brought him back in and got him settled with a favorite toy, I decided to go and see Sunny Cody, thereby ticking off the third thing on my to-do list for the day. While my primary reason for going to see Sunny Cody was to share what little information I was able to get from Beck Chandler, I also wanted to see how she was doing with her recovery.

She answered the door leaning on her crutches, but I could tell she was in quite a bit of discomfort.

"Hi. I just wanted to let you know how my talk with Beck Chandler went." I said.

She smiled and said, "Oh, and here I thought you were coming to check on me." She led the way to the living room, where she had her computer opened on the coffee table. Looking around, I noticed that a photo of her with her daughter Katie and one of her with her parents were tipped over on an end table, and the table itself was knocked crooked. The cane Tim, her PT, had given her was lying across the room near one of the baseboards. There was a small dent in the wall where I assumed the cane had bounced off it.

"Looks like your physical therapy is going well." I raised my eyebrows at her as I motioned to the discarded cane.

She sighed. "Well, it's going. Pretty damn slow, though. I hate this!" She banged one of her crutches down on the floor. She looked more upset than I had ever seen her.

"I know you want to speed things along, but pushing too fast is only going make it take longer to heal and get back to full function."

"You sound like Tim. Do they give all you medical people a script to read to patients or something?" She said.

"No. It's just a fact. It takes whatever time it takes for your body to heal."

She sighed and sat back, "Sorry I was being difficult. As I told my daughter, I'll behave and listen to doctor's orders now."

I thought the odds of that happening were probably fifty-fifty at best, but I said, "Good."

"Tell me how it went with Chandler," she said.

"He really didn't tell me anything. He denies being the one to give the pills to the boys that day. No surprise there, but as I was talking to him, Detective Langley showed up to question him also. As soon as he saw Langley approaching him, Chandler tried to run away, but stopped when the detective caught up with him. I was wondering what Detective Langley told you he found out."

"Langley questioned him?" She seemed surprised. "He never mentioned it to me. I'll put in a call and find out what he had to say. The captain agreed that I could be notified of any information they received, even if I am not supposed to be officially working the case anymore."

"When you call, maybe you can find out more about Beck Chandler's background, too. Evidently, he was accused of possessing narcotics with intent to sell several months ago, but then the drugs supposedly found in his possession disappeared, and the charges were dropped. He suffered a serious leg injury last year, and I would bet he received narcotic pain relievers during his recovery. I wondered if that could have gotten him involved with what is going on now." I made no mention of the parallels between her own injury and her refusal to take the pain meds prescribed for her.

She made a note on a pad sitting next to her computer. "I'll see what I can find out."

"Also, any more news on who might have been responsible for killing Mr. Bourne and injuring you?"

She shook her head, "Langley has been updating me on that investigation. The theory is the gang who was supposed to drop off the drugs to Bourne was tipped off he was cooperating with the police in a plea deal. The plan was changed then to eliminate Bourne before he could set them up to be arrested. Since the names Bourne gave us of the guys in the car delivering the drugs did not pan out, Langley is supposed to be following up on finding out who they were. He claims he's had no luck so far."

"How did you know Bourne wanted to share information with you that might have to do with your husband's killing?"

"He was arrested a few weeks before the incident on Windy Reed. He and three other guys were caught stealing catalytic converters from cars parked in one of the commuter lots. He had a long history of drug convictions and was looking at a long time incarcerated after this offense. He offered to make a deal to decrease the charges against him. Langley went to get the official okay, and I was alone with him for a few minutes. He never came right out and said what information he had, but he insinuated it would be of particular interest to me. I asked him what he meant by that, but Langley came back with the deal he was being offered, and Bourne shut up.

"What about the car that hit you? Do you think whoever killed him knew what he was going to tell you?"

"That's certainly possible."

I hesitated before I brought up another possibility. "You don't think that Bourne could have just been leading you on, that he made up the story just to get something else from you?"

"Yes. I thought of that, but something about the way he looked when he said he heard something I should know made me think he was telling the truth. He looked nervous for one thing. Not the usual smug look he had when he was arrested. Before one of the other officers took him away to finish the paperwork, he motioned toward his head and said, 'It's all up here.' I thought he just meant he had memorized the information."

I thought of the ball cap I had found. "Do you think he meant his hat?"

"It sounds crazy, and I never would have thought of that until you said you found his cap with writing in it. Not that it does us any good now."

I felt my stomach clench. It looked like maybe my car break-in wasn't a random act after all. "What about the other three men arrested with him? Could they be the ones who shot him? Were they out on bail?"

"One of them, Fred Blaine, made bail. It's possible. Langley says that Blaine never showed up to court, and his family claims not to know where he is."

I thought of something else, "Were you able to get any information on who might have brought in a car with front-end damage? Any luck with calling the body shops and garages?"

"First of all, there are more repair shops in the tri-town area than you can possibly imagine. Those I contacted either didn't have a record of such repairs based on our scant information or, as I expected, were keeping any information they might have close to their vest."

I had an idea how we might get some information, but I didn't want to say anything until I checked it out. "If you find out more on Beck Chandler, could you let me know? And if you want me to follow up on anything else, I'll be glad to do it."

Before I left, I retrieved her cane from across the room and handed it to her. "Listen to Tim's instructions. Be patient. I promise you'll get there."

Chapter Nineteen

I was looking forward to seeing my first patient the next day. Eighty-four-year-old Katherine Paine had been teetering on the edge of congestive heart failure for several months. So far medications had been enough to keep her condition in check, but her physician had concerns about how well she was following her low-salt diet and if she was exercising as he had advised her. I was checking on her to make sure her symptoms weren't worsening and to relay her vital signs to her doctor.

I always liked my visits to her because she was one of the nicest people I have had the pleasure to meet. She also was one of the most talkative. I usually allowed a bit of extra time when I scheduled a visit with her since she was never at a loss for topics of conversation. When she came to the door, I saw that while her color was good, she was not the perky pink she had been on my last visit. I also noticed her breathing was slightly labored as she had me follow her into her livening room.

When we were seated, I asked, "How are you feeling, Mrs. Paine?" I'd let her explain her symptoms as she saw them before I told her what I noticed.

"Well, okay, I guess. My darn feet and ankles are a bit puffy, though." She lifted both feet off the floor to show me. "Do you think Dr. Moore will be able to put me on a stronger dose of my diuretics to help that?"

"I'll let him know, and we'll see. First, why don't I check your blood pressure and listen to your lungs." Her blood pressure was on the high side of normal, and I noticed she had a slight wheeze when she spoke. I was not surprised at all that her lung sounds were coarser than when I had last checked on her. "You are having a little harder time breathing, aren't you?"

The fact that she nodded and just said "A bit" rather than going into a long explanation of when that symptom started and exactly what activities caused her to get out of breath told me she was definitely not herself.

"I am going to call your doctor before I leave and let him know what you told me and what I've observed. He'll decide if he needs to examine you right away or wait a few days to see if an increase in your medication doses make a difference." As I was hoping, he wanted her to come in the next day.

As I prepared to leave and was tucking my blood pressure machine and stethoscope back into my bag, Mrs. Paine said, "What's wrong, dear?"

I was startled by her question. "I'm sorry, what do you mean?"

"I can see something is bothering you. Of course, just go ahead and tell me if it's none of my business."

I didn't think my feelings of sadness and anger at Justin were showing. I didn't even think I still had those feelings. "It's nothing really. I just left a relationship, and that is on my mind, I guess." I smiled at her and said, "I 'll be fine, though."

She took my hand and squeezed it. "I know you will. Things will work out for the best; you'll see. In the meantime, take good care of yourself."

I said, "I will." and turned to go before she could see the tears that had welled up in my eyes. I was touched by her kind words. But I took extra care to make sure I was cheerful and upbeat with the remainder of the patients I saw that day.

On my way to my car after my last client of the day, I got a call from my next-door neighbor, Karen. I had hired her daughter, Jenny, to play with Bruno for a few minutes and take him out to do his business after she came home from school.

"Hi, Karen. Is everything all right with Bruno?"

"Yes, he's just great. Jenny took him out and then threw his ball for him for a while. I called because there is a strange car parked in front of your house."

My heart rate immediately sped up, "What does it look like? Is it cream-colored or light gray?"

"No. It's dark colored. Looks like black or dark blue. Were you expecting company? I don't want to be nosy or anything, but it seemed unusual for someone to just park in front of your house like that. It's been there for at least twenty minutes."

Karen *was* nosy, but I was glad of that. She had tipped me off to some dangerous situations in the past. "No, I wasn't expecting anyone. I'll be home soon. I'll find out what's going on."

The car was still there when I pulled into my driveway. It looked vaguely familiar, and I remembered where I had seen it before when Detective Langley stepped out from behind the wheel.

"Good evening, Miss Bass. May I speak with you a moment?"

I hoped he was here to let me know what Beck Chandler had told him, but I didn't think that was likely.

"Sure. Come on in." I could hear Bruno whining and barking on the other side of the door.

"I don't think that will be necessary," he said. "I just want to remind you that you are not empowered to interview witnesses or suspects in a crime. Detective Cody was seriously injured, so her judgment may be impaired, but you are not a police officer and so should stay out of any ongoing investigations." With that, he turned and headed back to his car.

"There is no law against me speaking to people if I want!" I shouted after him. He didn't respond. I immediately regretted that I couldn't think of something stronger to say to him, but his words had struck a tender spot. I had heard words very similar to those spoken by someone else recently. I comforted myself with the thought that I would just love to see what happened if Langley told Sunny Cody to her face that her judgment was impaired.

I was still irritated with Langley when I went into the house. Bruno was ecstatic at seeing me, as usual, so I tried to calm down by petting and playing with him. It worked, a little, but I could see why Sunny did not like the man. "Whatever happened to the police appreciating the help of the public in obtaining information?" I asked Bruno.

After I fed Bruno and started my own dinner, I sorted through the mail I had tossed on the counter. Mostly junk mail, until I came to the postcard with a happy looking dog and cat. They were dressed in scrubs and had a stethoscope around their neck. Even though I knew what it was, I turned it over to read the message: "It's that time again! Bruno is due for his annual physical exam and to update his vaccinations! Call to make his appointment today."

Great. I had just started to relax from my confrontation with Detective Langley. Now I tensed up at the thought that I would have to see Justin again sooner rather than later, and to worry about how that would go.

"I'll call the vet's office tomorrow, and I'll ask for an appointment with Dr. Reddy, not Dr. McKenzie, right?" I said to Bruno. He looked at me like he understood exactly what I was talking about, and not for the first time, I wished I really knew what dogs thought when we spoke to them.

Thinking about Justin made me remember Lynn's prediction that Alex Drover was about to propose at their special dinner the previous night. I wondered if she was correct. As if on cue, she called me.

"Hi, Melanie!"

She sounded happy, so that was a good sign. "Well?" I said.

"I was right! Wait 'til you see the ring! I really would like the wedding to be in spring. We don't have a date yet, but when we do, I want you to be my maid of honor. I don't have any family I'm close to, and you were instrumental in helping me start over here, so I hope you will say yes. Of course, Bruno can come if you want to bring him."

She was speaking very fast, and it was a little much to take in all at once, but I was glad she seemed so happy. "Of course. I'll be honored to be in your wedding."

"I realize you don't know Alex very well, so I'd love for you and Justin to meet us for dinner next week. I'm sure you'll like Alex once you get a chance to spend some time with him."

I took a deep breath before answering, "I'd love to meet you and Alex for dinner, but I'm afraid Justin and I are no longer seeing each other."

I heard her gasp. "What! Why? And you let me go on babbling about Alex and how we're getting married! I'm so sorry."

I told her about Justin's strong objection to my continuing to be involved in dangerous situations and my feeling that I did not want someone controlling the choices I made.

"Wow! I knew he didn't love you getting mixed up in Detective Cody's case, to be honest, it worries me a little also, but I didn't think he felt *that* strongly about it."

"I guess I underestimated his concerns, too."

"Give him time. Maybe he'll come to see your side of things."

I sighed, "I don't know about that." I felt bad squashing her excitement over her engagement and wanted to get back to a happier subject. "Let's concentrate on celebrating your good news. Does Alex's family live locally? Have you met any of them yet?"

"His parents are divorced, and his father remarried and lives in Key West. His mother lives in Westport. We're having dinner with her this weekend so I can meet her. I'm a bit nervous. I never realized just how wealthy his family is, but his mother comes from old New England stock. From what I heard, her name is always being mentioned in the society news and on social media, and that she chairs several charitable organizations." She laughed then, "I guess you could say she is an Influencer in the over sixty set."

"Well, her future daughter-in-law is an up-and-coming artist who her son loves, so don't let her intimidate you," I said.

"Thanks. I won't. And don't hesitate to call me if you want to talk about anything or if you need to vent your feelings."

After we ended our call, I realized what an emotional roller coaster of a day it had been, and how glad I was for it to end.

Chapter Twenty

I volunteered the following day to give flu shots at the Community Center in town. The pop-up clinic was being run by the Department of Public Health to make it easy for local residents to get their vaccinations in what promised to be a worse-than-usual flu season. Over the course of the day, I was glad to see a huge turnout. The organizers had anticipated this, and there were several health professionals giving the vaccinations, so we were able to move the lines along quickly.

The clinic was scheduled to close at four PM, and the crowd had thinned out when I noticed a group of three women standing near the exit of the room. One was Audrey Cullen, and the other two looked familiar, but I don't think I ever knew their names. They were deep in conversation. I wished they had gone to my station for their vaccinations so I could pick up any new nuggets of information about what was going on with their sons. Maybe something I could pass along to Sunny Cody. I began to put away my supplies, taking my time and trying to see if I could hear what they were discussing. Out of the corner of my eye, I saw someone approach them. Beth Forbes. Their discussion went on for a minute or so more, though judging by the change in their posture, I didn't think the other women were too thrilled by Beth intruding in their conversation. Suddenly there was no issue with hearing what was said.

Beth's voice was strident as she said, "I'm telling you, he is dangerous, and I don't want him around my son. I'm going over coach's head to the school board!"

"You have no evidence to prove he was involved in what happened." Audrey

Cullen stood with her arms crossed.

Beth huffed loudly, "Really? Don't tell me you haven't heard about what happened with him in the spring!" She turned to one of the other women, "And your son *found* the pills in the boys' restroom? Come on!"

The short, dark-haired woman jabbed a finger at Beth. "Are you insinuating Nick was lying? He would never lie about something as serious as that, and he swears..."

Their loud conversation was abruptly halted as one of the security guards rushed over to them. "Okay ladies, let's take your discussion outside." He ushered them out the door. It was all I could do not to stop packing up and rush out after them.

It seemed like Beth Forbes still felt Beck Chandler was behind distributing the illegal drugs. Now that I knew about his past troubles, I could see why she would think that.

On the way home, I thought again about what Audrey and her cohorts were talking about before I left. I wondered if Sunny had a chance to find out what Detective Langley had learned from Beck Chandler. Also, I agreed that Nick Meyers was holding back something about where he got the pills. His mother was certainly acting like a mama bear protecting her cub, but surely the police could try to question him again to see if he still told the same story.

I was bustling around my kitchen, gathering things to make my dinner, chatting away to Bruno when I glanced at the postcard from the veterinary practice reminding me to make his appointment. I sighed, stopped what I was doing, and dialed their number. I had been putting off doing it, but it was necessary. The practice was open until seven PM, so I knew someone would be there.

"Hi. This is Melanie Bass. I'd like to make an appointment with Dr. Reddy for Bruno's yearly physical."

"Melanie! This is Traci. Dr. Reddy is only in on Tuesdays and Thursdays now, but I guess you probably know that." She giggled. "Why don't I book Bruno with Dr. McKenzie on Monday."

My stomach clenched for a moment. "No. Not Dr. McKenzie. I'd rather see Dr Reddy, please."

She sounded a bit confused. "Oh. Okay. Well, he can see Bruno on Tuesday if that works for you."

"That's fine. See you then." I figured if Justin hadn't said anything about us breaking up, that gossip would certainly be around the practice now.

I had one more thing I wanted to do before I settled down for the evening. Sunny said she had had no luck in finding a body shop that might have repaired the car damaged by hitting her. But as she said, sometimes people were reluctant to talk to the police. I had one more idea. I knew someone who always seemed to have an extensive network of connections. I called Charlie Duggan.

"Hi, Charlie. How are you feeling this evening?"

"I'm alive, so I got no reason to complain. You need something? I'm guessing you didn't call just to ask me about my health."

"Detective Cody called the local body shops and garages to see if they had done a repair on a car that matches the description of the vehicle that hit her. She didn't have any luck. I was wondering if you know anybody that owns a body shop. Someone that might have done a repair on the car that hit Detective Cody. Someone that wouldn't hesitate to tell you. I realize I didn't give you much of a description, and it's a long shot."

He was quiet for several seconds, and I wasn't sure if he'd put the phone down. "Charlie? You there?"

"I'm trying to think. I know one guy for sure. He used to fix my old Buick, don't know if he's still in business, though. Another guy I used to play cards with turned the day-to-day operation of his shop over to his son-in-law, but he might be able to find out if the car we're looking for came in for repair in the past few weeks. I'll ask around and see if I can find out anything."

I smiled, even though he couldn't see me. "Thank you. I knew I could count on you."

"Course, we're assuming that if they did get the car repaired that they did it local," he said.

"True, but maybe we'll get lucky."

"Yup. We'll see."

Chapter Twenty-One

The weekend was thankfully quiet. I took advantage of the good weather to get the remainder of the yard work done. That is, I raked leaves, and Bruno dove into the piles and redistributed them. The physical activity of raking and the joy I felt watching Bruno dive and tunnel into them was very relaxing. I was able to just concentrate on the here and now and put all my worries aside.

On Monday, I called Lynn at lunchtime to find out how her dinner with Alex's mother went. "How did it go with Mrs. Drover? Was she as formidable as you feared?"

Lynn laughed, but she sounded tense. "No, not formidable, but not terribly warm either. At least she seemed rather aloof to me."

"What do you mean?"

"She obviously was thrilled to see Alex, and she insisted I call her Diana, so everything started off fine. She asked polite questions about where I was from and how I liked working at High Life Dermatology as a receptionist. Though, the way she said receptionist let me know what she thought of that position. Alex told her about my painting and that I taught art classes, but I didn't get the feeling that she was very interested in hearing about my job and my art. What she *was* particularly interested in was what brought me to Connecticut and why I stayed."

"That sounds like it could have been an awkward question to answer," I said.

"It was. Alex said he told her that I had been married before, so I just explained I had come for Artie's funeral. I know I shouldn't have felt embarrassed since I wasn't the only one with a failed marriage. Among the three of us, we have a quartet of ex-spouses. Though, of course, there is the sordid fact that one of mine was involved in illegal activities and subsequently murdered. I'm not even sure why she asked since what happened to Artie was all over the news. Anyway, I think it was the why I stayed part that interested her more." Lynn took a deep breath, "Alex said not to mind how his mother behaved. He said she was just very protective and that she would come to love me as she got to know me better. I certainly got the message about her being protective, but honestly, the man is forty-two years old and seems capable of taking care of himself."

I chuckled, "I see your point, but as he said, I'm sure she'll begin to relax as she gets to know you better. It is only the first time you've met."

"That's just it, though. As much as I love Alex, I find something about the woman off-putting. I think it may take some time for me to warm up to her, also."

That was a problem. One I hoped wouldn't interfere with her relationship with Alex. "Give it time. After all, you both love Alex."

"That's true. Speaking of which, why don't you meet us for dinner tomorrow night? I'd love for you to get to know him better."

"Yes. That would be great. I'd like that."

"Still no word from Justin? Are you sure you can't work things out?"

I found it didn't hurt as much to talk about it now. "No, it doesn't look that way."

"I have a class to teach in half an hour, so I need to go, but just remember, you never know how things may turn out."

I remembered what Mrs. Paine had said about things working out for the best, and deep down, I realized I still held out hope also. "Thanks for the encouragement."

After work, I needed to stop at the local Stop and Shop for groceries and Bruno's dog food. I ran into Audrey Cullen in the produce section. She was picking up tomatoes and inspecting them and then slamming them down a bit harder than I thought was advised for such easily bruised fruit.

"Hello, Audrey. Is everything all right?

She startled when I spoke to her, but then gently placed the tomato in her hand back in the display. "Oh hi, yes everything is fi.... No. Everything is not all right! Tyler was suspended from school for three days for fighting."

She looked as if she was about to cry, but it was hard to tell if it was from sorrow or anger.

"What happened? Why was he fighting?"

"It's that Beth Forbes' fault. Actually, it's her son's. Someone slashed two of Beth's tires over the weekend, and her son blamed Tyler and his friends. He said they did it to get back at her because she planned to go to the school board to request Beck Chandler be fired. Tyler denied doing it, and they got into a fight."

"I'm sorry to hear that. Do you think it's possible that the boys may have had something to do with it?"

I prepared myself for an immediate angry denial, but instead, she hesitated just a moment, then said, "Anna Meyers said the boys were at her house, hanging out in Nick's room on Saturday night. Besides, even though Beth seems to enjoy stirring up trouble, the boys would never do something like that."

I hoped she was right. If it wasn't Tyler and his friends, though, who did do it? It seemed like more than a coincidence it happened after Beth made her threat. I wondered if Beck had heard about her plans.

According to our local newspaper, the boys' soccer team had made the playoffs. Their first game was set to be played on their home field in two days. I thought about stopping by and seeing if I got an opportunity to speak with Beck Chandler again. This time on a fishing expedition to see what he knew about the vandalism to Beth Forbes's car. It seemed to me that he would be foolish to commit such a petty crime if he wanted to stay off the police department's radar. But maybe, if Tyler and his friends did have anything to do with it, they would have told Chandler so he knew they were "sticking up" for him. I thought of Detective Langley's warning to me to stay out of police business. That made me want to question Chandler even more.

Chapter Twenty-Two

Bruno was very excited the next day when I grabbed his leash and led him toward the car. I was not nearly as excited. I told myself there was no need to be nervous. I was bringing Bruno to see Dr. Reddy. I probably wouldn't even have an opportunity to run into Justin. If I did, I'd smile and wave, then look away.

As I approached the front desk, I saw that it was the practice's part-time receptionist, Kerri, working today. She smiled, and her eyes lit up as she saw Bruno.

She scooted around the desk and knelt to pet him. "Hi, sweet boy! Look at you!"

Bruno hopped around and wagged his whole body, washing Kerri's hands with kisses.

I said, "Is Dr. Reddy all set to see him, or should we take a seat?"

Kerri went back behind the desk and said, "Oh, yeah, I'm sorry, but Dr. Reddy wasn't feeling well today, so he's out. Dr. McKenzie can see Bruno, though. Just have a seat, and he'll be right with you."

She must have seen the stricken look on my face because she said, "Is that all right? I didn't want to cancel, and since Dr. McKenzie has seen Bruno before, I thought it would be fine."

I told myself it was stupid to just turn around and leave, and really it was all about Bruno and his well-being. That did little to calm the tight feeling in my stomach, however. "Okay. Sure, that will be fine." I perched on the edge of a chair, holding Bruno's leash so tight I had white knuckles.

Once we were led to an examination room, I found myself fidgeting on the bench and lifted Bruno into my lap to try to calm my nerves. That only lasted a few minutes, however, since as soon as the exam room door opened and Justin walked in, Bruno was off my lap in a shot and dancing around his feet.

Justin lifted Bruno up, murmuring something to him I couldn't hear, then looked at me. "Hi, Melanie. It's nice to see the two of you today." He then broke eye contact and seemed to be looking everywhere but at me.

I was glad to see that despite his casual greeting he seemed as unsure of how to act as I did. "Yes, nice to see you also."

He nodded and placed Bruno on the exam table. "Okay, let's see how this guy is doing."

I stood by the table, one hand on Bruno as Justin did his exam. As he gently squeezed Bruno's belly and checked his ears, he said, "So, everything going all right with you? Are you doing well?"

"Yes. Fine. And you?" It was strange to have such a formal conversation with someone with whom, up until recently, I had had a much more intimate relationship. When Artie and I divorced, our conversations weren't particularly deep, but certainly, there was an undercurrent of emotion. Usually anger and disappointment on my part.

"Well, I'm happy to say he's in excellent health." As Justin spoke, he placed his hand over mine where it rested on Bruno's back, but as if he suddenly realized what he had done, he just as quickly pulled it away.

I felt a brief jolt of emotion when he touched my hand- comfort? Longing? I fought to keep my reaction from showing.

"Any issues or questions you have for me?" Justin suddenly looked flustered. "About Bruno, I mean."

We both started to laugh, and I saw him blush.

"No, he's been acting fine," I said.

"Good. I'll just give him the vaccination updates he needs." After he was done, he patted Bruno's head and scratched his ears. He looked at me again and said, "I'll see you. Be sure to call if you have any concerns."

It wasn't a particularly warm day, but when I left the veterinarian practice, I felt as sweaty and drained as if I'd run a half marathon. As I buckled Bruno in his harness again, I said, "Well, that was not what I expected! But, as usual, you were a good boy, Bruno." It hadn't been as bad seeing Justin again as I first feared. Though, the fact that I kept going over in my mind what he said, how he acted, how I responded, made me feel like I was back in middle school.

That afternoon Bruno was acting a little punky. I knew from experience that it was most likely due to the vaccines he had gotten that morning, but I thought of calling Lynn to cancel dinner with her and Alex for that evening. After a few hours, however, Bruno perked up, and I decided to go ahead with my plans.

Lynn had chosen a new restaurant in town. One that fell between outrageously overpriced and family fare, though leaning more toward the overpriced side. As I entered, the smell of garlic, tomatoes, and roasting meat wafted out, and I hoped the food was as good as it smelled. I liked the fact that the floor plan allowed for quiet little nooks where conversations would not be overheard and a few tables out in the open that could be combined for larger parties. I wasn't sure what name Lynn had used to make the reservation, but it was no matter because she waved me over as soon as I arrived. Lynn and Alex were nestled into one of the corner alcoves.

Though I had seen Alex before, I had never really paid much attention to his looks. At the time I had met him, Lynn and I were deeply involved in solving the murder of our mutual ex-husband, Artie Krapaneck. Lynn was right. Alex was handsome in a very clean-cut way. Sandy hair, blue eyes, clean-shaven strong jaw. Not really my type, though. I flashed on Justin's rumpled dark hair and five o'clock shadow.

After our initial greetings and placing our drink orders, we exchanged pleasantries, and all agreed the restaurant had been an excellent choice.

Conversation had lagged for a moment, so I asked, "How do you like working at High Life Dermatology, Alex?"

"I really enjoy it. I came from a much smaller, slightly more elite practice in Westport. I like the wider variety of patients we see at High Life."

Lynn gave him a slight nudge, "I notice that quite a lot of our young female patients request their appointments with you."

Alex grinned, "And I notice you often book them to see Dr. Wang or Dr. Devlin."

"Well, I think it's only fair we balance the type of patients seen between all of the doctors," Lynn said.

After we finished our meals, we were all quiet again until Lynn said, "How is that case going with Detective Cody?" She turned to Alex, "Remember I told you Melanie was involved in another crime investigation?"

"I'm not exactly investigating the crime, just following up on some leads for her while she's out injured." It struck me that I had been doing a lot of denying about being involved in the investigation, but it was time to admit, at least to myself, that I was. "I think that we are making some progress." I didn't feel comfortable mentioning any specifics in front of Alex, though I might run a few things by Lynn later.

"How about you? No more problems with your neighbor, are there?"

Lynn looked slightly uncomfortable for a moment, "No. Probably not." She looked at Alex, "I think I'm just reading into everything lately, but it looked like someone had rifled through my mail yesterday. The mail carrier usually stacks it neatly in my mailbox, but it looked kind of scattered when I went to get it. I even found one piece, thankfully just an advertisement, lying on the ground under the mailbox."

Alex took another fork full of his tiramisu. "Huh. You could have a new mail carrier, one who isn't as meticulous as your former one."

He was right, it could have a logical explanation, but since Lynn had been questioning someone stalking her, I found her disturbed mail a bit suspicious. Alex didn't seem overly concerned, or even concerned at all.

"Why do you think someone would go through your mail?" I asked.

Lynn shook her head, "I have no idea."

Alex asked for a refill of his coffee when the server came to check on us, then said, "So I hear you are going to be Lynn's maid of honor at our wedding." He took Lynn's hand as he spoke.

I was a little jolted by the change in subject, as if he found the idea of a stalker not worthy of discussion. I decided not to make a big deal of it now, but I would certainly find a way to question Lynn about his attitude later.

I took a sip of water to compose myself. "Yes. I was so happy she asked me. I have to say, though, you two have had quite a whirlwind romance. Lynn says that you'll probably get married in the spring?" I looked at Lynn for confirmation, but she was gazing lovingly at Alex. I decided it would be better if I didn't harp on the speed with which they were engaged. She did have until spring to be sure.

"Sure, if that's what Lynn wants. Though my mother said if we can wait until next fall, we can use her villa in Provence for our honeymoon."

The offer of a trip to France certainly sounded like a wonderful honeymoon, but I could see by the look on Lynn's face that she was not terribly excited about it.

She began fiddling with her cup of tea. "I know that is a generous offer, but I really had my heart set on a spring wedding. Besides, didn't you honeymoon in that villa after your first marriage?"

He gave her a lopsided grin, "Yeah, but France…" He put his arm around her and gave her a one-armed hug.

Lynn gave him a tight smile and shrugged his arm off her shoulders. "Maybe we can talk about it later."

I was thankful they both let the subject drop after that, and I immediately started thinking of a way I could diplomatically and honestly give Lynn my opinion of Alex when she asked. He did seem to be in love with her, yet he seemed a bit clueless about her feelings, and I found I didn't really trust him.

Chapter Twenty-Three

The next morning, I received a text from Sunny Cody: **Any free time this afternoon?**

I was scheduled to see my last patient at three PM, so texted back that I would be able to stop by her house at 3:45. I was curious to see if Langley had gotten back to her with what he learned from Beck Chandler and if she heard who had been responsible for the vandalism at Beth Forbes's house.

When I rang Sunny's doorbell, the door was opened by her four-year-old daughter, Katie.

She immediately said, "Hi, Miss Bass! Guess what! I'm doing a sleepover at grandma's!"

I was glad to see she had lost the worried look she had the last time I saw her.

She stepped away from the door to let me enter, then continued, "Tomorrow, she is taking me to see the bones! She says there's going to be lots and lots of bones!"

I was saved from trying to guess what that meant when Sunny's mother came into the foyer, putting on her jacket and carrying an overnight bag. She handed Katie her jacket and said, "You'll have to excuse us, Miss Bass. Someone is very excited at the prospect of seeing the dinosaurs at the Peabody Museum of Natural History tomorrow." She turned briefly to look behind her where I could hear Sunny approaching, and said to me, "Good luck" as she and Katie left.

I was surprised to see that Sunny was also wearing a jacket as she hobbled into the entranceway using her crutches.

"What...?"

"I feel like getting some fresh air. Do you mind if we take a ride? You drive." Motioning to the cane resting against a chair, she said, "Could you grab that for me? I'm going to need it later."

I was glad to see she felt up to going out for a while, but I was thoroughly mystified as to what was going on and why she asked me to drive her. "I'm glad to help you out, but I'm sure your mother would have been happy to drive you and Katie around for a bit. Is there a reason you asked me to do it?"

"Yes. Help me get into the car, and I'll explain."

I pulled the front passenger seat of my Subaru as far back as it would go and turned to help her into the car. She grunted as she tried to get her leg in a comfortable position. "Maybe we should have taken my Jeep; there is a bit more legroom."

"We can change cars if you like." I was tempted to add that she was the one who planned this expedition, whatever it was.

"No. I'm settled now. Let's go."

"Where are we going?"

"To have a little talk with Eric Meyers. Greg Langley says he questioned Eric about the vandalism to Beth Forbes's car. Eric insists he didn't do it and knows nothing about it. His mother swore he was home all night so couldn't have been involved. Langley said he thinks they are both lying but couldn't get Eric to admit to anything."

"What about Tyler Cullen? He claims to be innocent also, according to Audrey Cullen."

"Let's start with Eric and see what we find out."

As I backed out of her driveway, Sunny gave me the Meyers's address. "I have the feeling that you're interested in talking to Eric about more than slashing tires," I said.

"Yes, I never got out of Greg Langley exactly where in the boy's bathroom Eric found the pills they took. Either he never found out, or Eric gave him a full explanation, and Langley just isn't sharing. It will be interesting to find out if I get the same story he told before."

"What does Detective Langley say about you going to speak to the Meyers boy?" I hadn't told Sunny about his warning to me to stay out of police business.

"I didn't bother to tell him. If I do find out something that helps the investigation, I'll let him know, and he can follow up. Not that I want to have him given credit he doesn't deserve."

My guess was that even if we found out something useful, Detective Langley would not accept the information gracefully. I also didn't think Sunny cared what he thought about us following up with our own investigation.

The Meyers lived in a house down a narrow winding road. I noted only two other houses set far back from the road as we approached. "Tyler said Nick doesn't drive yet; how far is it to where Beth Forbes lives? Seems like it would be a long way to walk."

I heard her take a sharp breath as she shifted her position in the seat to try to reach the cane in the back seat. She gave up after two attempts. "Friends. A couple of the boys in that group have their driver's license."

That made sense, and in spite of his denial, I was willing to bet Audrey's son Tyler was one of the boys with him.

My first instinct, and what I certainly hoped she had in mind, was for me to go in with her as she spoke to the Meyers. However, I did ask. "Should I wait here or....?"

Sunny sighed and said, "Normally, I would say yes. I'm skating on thin ice letting you get even more involved, but I think I need your help." She motioned to her leg. "I'll question him, though. I just want you to watch and listen. Let me know what you think about what he tells me."

I rushed around to help her out of the car. As I reached for her crutches, she said, "No. Hand me the cane. I don't want to look too fragile."

Judging by how unstable she looked as she took her first few steps, she was going to have to put on quite an act. "No. I'll get your crutches. I'm afraid you're going to fall, and that will do nothing to add to your credibility, never mind what it will do to your knee."

She stopped to take a few deep breaths, then said, "No. I can do this."

She did seem a bit steadier as we got to the front door, but I walked closely by her side just in case. Since she was several inches taller than me, we would both go down if she started to fall, however. I held my breath as she struggled to maneuver the steps up to the front door, but again she waved off my offer of help.

As soon as Anna Meyers answered the door, Sunny took out her badge and said, "Hello. I'm Detective Cody. I wonder if I could have a word with your son."

I could see Anna give me a questioning look, and Sunny motioned to me and said, "This is Ms. Bass. She's my driver."

I was sure Mrs. Meyers recognized me from both the day the boys overdosed and from the vaccine clinic, but she didn't question my presence any further. She turned her attention back to Sunny. "An officer was already here to speak to Nick; why do you need to talk to him again?"

"I just want to follow up on something. May we?"

I saw a fine sweat begin to form on Sunny's forehead and thought that if Mrs. Meyers didn't let us in and offer Sunny a seat soon, I was fairly sure she was going to collapse on their doorstep.

"Okay. But I will be right there with him when you question him," she said.

"Of course." Sunny slowly settled into what looked like the firmest of the easy chairs in the living room.

I looked around as Mrs. Meyers went to get Nick from his room. I noticed several pictures of her with Nick, Nick with an older boy who looked like it must be a brother, and Nick with several of the boys on his soccer team. I saw no pictures of anyone who looked like he was Nick's father.

I heard voices coming from upstairs. One was Mrs. Meyers, and then it sounded like two deeper voices. One of the deeper voices sounded annoyed. I was unable to make out what they were saying, though.

I was surprised to see that when Nick and his mother came into the living room, Tyler Cullen was with them. The boys sank down next to each other on the sofa. Both sat with their hands on their knees, their feet flat on the floor in a mirror image of each other. My first thought was that they were taller than I remembered, but then I hadn't met them under the best of circumstances, either. I noticed Nick kept moving his left foot, so his leg bounced up and down. Tyler fisted and then opened his hands several times, then seemed to be aware of what he was doing and stopped, placing his hands back on his knees.

Mrs. Meyers sat in a chair close to the sofa, and while she appeared to be giving Sunny her full attention, I could see her taking quick side glances toward the boys.

Sunny started to say, "Nick, I was wondering..."

"Look, if this is about what happened to Luke's mom's car, I already said I didn't have anything to do with it! How many times is somebody going to ask me?" He looked at Tyler. "Tyler was with me the night they say it happened. We were in my room playing video games all evening. Right?"

Tyler nodded, but I saw his eyes dart briefly to Mrs. Meyers.

Sunny was silent for a few seconds, then said, "What I was going to say was, I'm curious to know exactly where in the boys' bathroom you found the pills you took that day during the soccer game."

Nick reached up to scratch his chin. "Oh. Um, they were taped under one of the sinks. I dropped my phone, and when I bent to pick it up, I saw them." He paused for a moment and quickly glanced at his mother. "I don't know who put them there. There are like a million kids that use that restroom every day. It could have been anyone."

I was sure it wasn't lost on Sunny that his explanation sounded rehearsed. I noticed also that Tyler was staring at the floor during Nick's recital of how he came by the drugs, and Mrs. Meyers was looking with what appeared to be approval at her son.

She saw me watching her, and she took on a concerned expression. "He's right. I know there have been issues with students caught with drugs at school before. There was a big deal made at the last PTO meeting of how despite the school and the community claiming to crack down on drug use, things like this still happen. Nick must have stumbled on some pills meant for someone else." She gave the boys a stern look, "Though I'm not excusing Nick, or Tyler, for what they did."

Sunny shifted in her chair, repositioning her leg. I could see she was getting uncomfortable, but she continued with her questions. "So, who do you think might have left those pills there?"

Nick shrugged and frowned, "Like I said, no idea." He looked at Tyler.

Tyler shook his head, "Yeah, I don't know."

"You are friends with Coach Chandler, aren't you? Did he ever talk with you about kids who might be using drugs?"

They looked at each other, then Nick said, "No."

"Did he maybe offer to hook you up with some pills?"

"No!" Nick straightened up from the slouched position he had drifted into. "I didn't get those pills from Beck."

I had a lot of experience when I was a nurse on a med-surg floor in dealing with people who were suspected of using illegal drugs. There usually was something in the way they phrased their denial, or a tell in their body language that tipped you off that they were lying. I didn't sense anything like that with Nick. For the first time since he had started answering questions, I believed what Nick was saying. Most of the rest of what he told Sunny seemed laced with lies.

Tyler shook his head and said, "No way! He wouldn't do that."

Anna Meyers looked indignant, though there was something in her expression that didn't ring true. "Nick's told you the truth, detective, and I'd appreciate it if you would stop harassing him. He made a mistake. We all make mistakes. As for Beck Chandler, it seems to me that you people are harassing him also, and you should look elsewhere to find out where all these kids are getting drugs."

Sunny looked at her and said, "How about you, Mrs. Meyers? Do you know of or have you heard of anyone who might be responsible for distributing the drugs?"

She stood up abruptly, a flush of pink starting to crawl up her neck. "Of course not! I think you've asked enough questions for now, and if there is a next time you want to question my son or me, I will speak to my lawyer first."

Sunny managed to get up out of her chair without too much difficulty, but I could tell by how pale she looked that it would take all the strength she had left to make it back to the car. "If you do think of anything that could help the investigation, please give me a call." She placed her card on a side table as we left.

I helped Sunny back into the car, and I waited a minute or two after we left the Meyers before I said, "That was...interesting. I have to say I'm inclined to believe Nick didn't get the pills from Beck Chandler after all, but I also don't believe he found those drugs either."

Sunny nodded. "I agree. It was also interesting how all three of them jumped to defend Chandler."

I had a sudden thought. "Too bad you didn't ask Mrs. Meyers if *she* was home the night Beth Forbes's tires were slashed."

"Good question. You aren't so bad at this investigation stuff." She sat silently for a while, then said, "I realize something else now, too. I'm in no shape to do leg work yet. No pun intended."

When we got to Sunny's, I offered to help her into the house. It looked like she was about to refuse, but then she said, "Okay. Thank you." She hoisted herself onto her crutches, and I grabbed her cane from the back seat.

"I'll just walk beside you, make sure you don't lose your balance. Tell me if you need to stop and rest a second."

She nodded and started toward her house. She seemed steady enough but went slower than I had seen her walking for some time.

My plan was to walk with her to see that she was able to make it up her front steps and into the house all right. She had just entered the house and turned to say something to me when I heard a sound like a firecracker. The potted purple chrysanthemum by my feet exploded, and I felt a sharp pain in my right ankle. Sunny grabbed my arm and yanked me inside, shutting the door behind us in what seemed like one motion. I fought to regain my balance once I was inside.

"Are you hurt?" Sunny had lost one crutch in the commotion, but hobbled over to pull aside the corner of the drape at the front window and peek out to see if there was still someone out there.

I looked down to see that my pant leg was starting to soak with blood, but I was otherwise okay. "I'm all right." My voice came out as a squeak. "What was that? Did someone shoot at us?"

She nodded, "Yes, it looks that way." She looked at my leg in alarm. "You're bleeding! Did they hit you?"

My hands shook as I pulled up my pant leg to see a two-inch gash above my ankle bone. "No, I don't think so. I think I was hit by flying pottery." I looked more closely at the cut, "I don't think it's too deep." My legs were trembling, so I went into her bathroom to try to calm down and clean my wound. After washing out the gash on my ankle, I grabbed a clean hand towel to press over it since it was still bleeding.

"I'll buy you a new one," I said as I walked back into the living room, motioning to the ruined towel.

Sunny was on her cell phone and waved my offer away. "Okay, I appreciate it, Frank. Thanks." She ended her call and then looked at me. "They are going to send someone right out to take our statement. He said there was an accident earlier on Route 79, and both lanes are closed. There are several officers at the scene there, and Frank said he'll pull somebody from there to come and talk to us now." She looked at my injured ankle again. "Are you sure you're going to be all right?"

I checked my wound. It was just seeping a small amount of blood now. "Yes. I have some steri-strips in my kit in the car. I think I can close it with those." I thought of the gunshot that seemed to come out of nowhere. "Maybe I'll wait until the officer gets here though to get my stuff out of the car."

Sunny said, "Did you see anyone right before this happened?"

"No. I was concentrating on making sure you made it into the house. Besides, I'm not familiar enough with your neighborhood to notice anyone who doesn't belong."

She sighed. "I didn't see anything either; like you said, I was trying not to fall on my butt."

She was rubbing her injured leg now.

"Did you hurt yourself again when you pulled me inside like that?" I asked.

"It didn't hurt at the time, but I guess I put a little too much weight on my leg when I lunged for the door. Would you be able to get me some Tylenol out of the medicine cabinet in the bathroom?"

CHAPTER TWENTY-THREE

I was returning with the bottle of medication, when I saw a police car pull into the driveway. That was a lot faster than I expected. I recognized the officer who got out as Officer Bridges. I met him earlier in the year when my house was broken into. He took a few minutes to look around before he approached the house, and when he reached the shattered flowerpot, he used his pen to sift through the dirt. It looked like he was checking for something in the soil. I yanked the door open before he could ring the bell.

As I let him in, he must have seen my stained pant leg. He said, "Is that blood yours?"

I looked down again and noticed a small tear in the fabric below the blood stain. "Yes. It's a minor injury, though." I pointed to the living room, "Detective Cody is in here."

He nodded to Sunny as he entered the room, and she motioned him to a chair. We both recounted what had happened when we got home and the fact that neither of us had seen or heard anything before being shot at. I knew our lack of information would probably mean we might never find out who was responsible.

Officer Bridges asked, "Are you sure it was a gunshot, not maybe a thrown rock, or like you said, maybe a firework somebody threw?"

Sunny glared at him. "I know what a gunshot sounds like."

He nodded. "Okay. Where did you say you were coming from when this happened?"

Sunny hesitated a second before answering. "I needed to get out of the house for a little while. Ms. Bass was kind enough to drive me while I ran an errand."

I thought at first Officer Bridges was going to ask exactly what this errand was, but after a brief hesitation, he continued with his other questions.

"Can you think of any reason someone might have been firing at you or your house?"

Sunny shook her head, "Do people even need a reason these days?"

"Yeah, you have a point." He put away the small pad he had been using to take notes. "Miss Bass, are you sure you don't want to get medical attention?"

"No. I'm fine," I said.

"Okay, then I'll file the report." He turned to Sunny, "You know what to do if you notice anything unusual or have any other problems."

After he left, I said to Sunny, "Could it have just been an accident, someone fooling around with a gun?"

"Bullets flying around in a residential neighborhood like that? I'd still be worried. But, no, I don't think that was an accident. However, I don't think whoever did it meant to hit us either."

"So, you think it may have been a warning of some kind? But why? You're a police detective; it's your job to ask questions and dig into people's business."

"I know." She glanced at me, "But it isn't your job to be involved."

I thought of Justin insisting on the same thing, and for a split second, I almost thought he might have a point.

"Maybe I shouldn't have gotten you involved in this investigation," Sunny said.

The fear I felt at being shot at turned to anger. Instead of being scared off by what happened, I felt irate. Now it was even more personal to me. "No. I was there when that car hit you, I had to resuscitate someone who almost died of a drug overdose, and now someone else could have shot one of us whether that was their intent or not. I am involved in this case no matter what." I was shaking by the time I finished my little speech, but I felt better. Except for my ankle, which had started to throb terribly.

I thought Sunny looked relieved, but she said, "All right. But if anything else happens that puts you in danger, you need to back off."

"Agreed." I didn't know if I would stick to that deal, but thought I'd wait and see before I decided. I had been through worse before.

Over Sunny's protests, I insisted on cleaning up the dirt and shattered flowerpot before I left. I checked again in the soil for a bullet before I swept it away but didn't see one. On the way home, I found myself unusually aware of any cars traveling behind me, but no one seemed to be following me.

I felt a flood of guilt as I pulled into my driveway. It was past Bruno's usual dinner time, and I wondered how long it had been since Jenny had been over to let him out. As I approached my door, I could see a note pinned to it:

"I didn't see your car here, so I fed Bruno and walked him again. I hope that is

all right. Jenny."

I felt thankful to have found such a great dog walker.

After quickly greeting Bruno, I went to change and care for my ankle wound. I was glad I had recently had my tetanus shot updated. I cleaned it again and was able to close it with three steri-strips. As I cleaned up, I mulled over who would want to frighten either Sunny or me off from talking to Nick Meyers and his mother. The whole tire-slashing incident was serious but not serious enough to warrant someone shooting at us. If someone had been following us to her house, I don't think either Sunny or I would have noticed, since we both were preoccupied with what had gone on at the Meyers's house.

Chapter Twenty-Four

I found it difficult to fall asleep that night. I tried not to toss and turn since Bruno was snuggled in his usual spot by my side, but I failed miserably. After a while, he got up and went to curl up at the foot of the bed. I took some Tylenol for the pain in my ankle, where the exploding flowerpot had not only cut me but must have also caused a deep bruise. It wasn't only my ankle keeping me awake, however. I kept thinking about what had gone on at the Meyers. I would have thought Nick's mother would want to know where exactly he got the drugs that could have killed him. I wasn't sure she believed him any more than we did. Maybe she was afraid to know the answer and afraid her son was more deeply involved in what was going on than she imagined.

I finally drifted off to sleep and groaned when my alarm went off in the morning. I gingerly moved my ankle to see how bad it felt, but it was not as painful as it had been the night before. I called in to the main office to speak to Judy, my supervisor, and explain that I had had a little accident and to ask if I could finish seeing patients a bit early. My wounded ankle was a legitimate excuse, but I also wanted to see if I could make it to the championship game at the soccer field.

I literally limped through my day, causing me to have to explain to each of my patients what had happened. I thought it best to just say I injured it doing work around the house. While that was not true, it seemed better than admitting what had really happened, although I was sure they would have found the real story infinitely more interesting. I took some over the counter pain killer at lunchtime and felt much better by the time I finished seeing my patients for the day. I went home to change out of my work clothes before going to the soccer game.

By the time I got there, the game was already underway. The parking lot at the field was filled, so I had to park in a line of cars pulled up onto the grass alongside the lot. I had given up hope of ever happening upon the car involved in Sunny's hit-and-run, so I didn't bother checking cars for damage and just headed right for the field. I could hear a lot of cheering and hoped it meant that we were winning. I wasn't sure I'd get a chance to speak to Beck Chandler after the game, no matter how it went, but I thought I'd give it a try. If nothing else, maybe I could figure out why Tyler, Nick, and their mothers were so sure he wasn't involved in the whole drug incident. His name kept coming up when it was discussed.

The game was nearly over, and I was glad to see that it did look like the home team was winning. I hoped to avoid running into the mothers I knew, at least for a while. I didn't want them to see me talking to Chandler. I slipped onto an end bleacher seat and looked around to be sure neither Audrey Cullen nor Anna Meyers was sitting nearby. Satisfied that I blended in the crowd, I searched the sidelines for Beck Chandler. I saw Coach Randall pacing back and forth, cheering, and clapping the shoulder of one of the boys on the bench as his team scored a goal. There was another guy; he looked like he might be someone's father, standing there also. His arms were raised in celebration. I didn't see Beck Chandler. A group of parents were gathered off to the side of the field, and I thought I saw Audrey among them. Maybe Chandler was talking with them, although I would have thought he'd be with the coach yelling encouragement to the team. I heard a loud cheer and looked back at the game to see someone streaking down the field in full control of the ball. It was Tyler Cullen. I had to admit that even though I didn't know a whole lot about soccer, I could tell the kid was good. Really good.

Tyler scored the final goal, and as the whistle blew, the bleachers around erupted in cheers. I watched the players hug each other and slap each other on the back and then line up to shake hands with the opposing team. The coaches also approached each other to shake hands, but still no Beck

Chandler.

I waited until the crowd had thinned out, and Coach Randall was no longer surrounded by parents offering congratulations before I approached him. "Hi coach, I'm Melanie Bass. I don't know if you remember me. The day we met was kind of crazy."

He held out a hand, "Oh, believe me, I remember you. I never got a chance to thank you for what you did that day. I was kind of rattled after what happened." He shook his head, "What a terrible thing. I think those boys learned a very difficult lesson, though. They are good boys. Hard to keep kids away from stuff like that these days."

"Yes. I'm not a parent myself, but as a nurse, I often see the damage illegal drug use can do."

He nodded and then said, "What can I do for you today?"

"I just wanted to say what a great game it was. Congratulations." I paused, "I didn't see Assistant Coach Chandler here. Too bad if he had to leave early and miss the end of the game."

Coach Randall bent to pick up his clipboard off the bench. "Beck Chandler never showed up for the game." I could see a look of disappointment on his face. "I'm not sure what happened."

"I heard some of the parents didn't want him coaching the boys. Something about problems he had with the police last spring?"

His nostrils flared, and he took a deep breath, "I'd say that maybe those people should take a good look at their own pasts. I think most of us are guilty of some sort of stupidity in our lives. What Beck was accused of was serious, but it was never proven that he did what they alleged he did. I've never had reason to suspect Beck was supplying drugs to any of the students in the school. And I've been watching, heaven help me." He looked directly at me then. "I'm a firm believer in second chances."

I gave him a beat to calm down, then I said, "So you haven't heard that the school board fired him or anything?"

"No. Nothing like that." He looked a bit uncomfortable now. "You'll have to excuse me I'm afraid. I am supposed to meet the team and their parents for pizza to celebrate the win."

I felt bad having ruined the coach's good mood. I was, however, curious why Beck Chandler never showed up for such an important game.

I texted Cody telling her about Chandler being a no-show, and asking if she could get me his address so I could go to talk to him at his apartment. By the time Sunny got back to me, I was home, and it was dark, so I decided to wait until the following day.

Chapter Twenty-Five

I waited until mid-afternoon to go to Chandler's house, assuming he might have class earlier in the day. According to the address Sunny gave me, he lived in an apartment on Fitch Street, not far from the college itself. There was one large apartment building on the same street as his address, but most of the street was lined with mid-twentieth-century multifamily homes. It turned out that he lived on the first floor of a three-floor walk-up that had been turned into student housing. I rang the bell marked Lowell/Chandler, and after several minutes, a slight, dark-haired young man dressed in a Super Mario T-shirt and sweatpants answered the door. He was barefoot and smelled strongly of weed.

"Hi. Are you Mr..." I leaned back to look at the name next to the bell again, "Lowell?"

"Yeah, I'm Benjy Lowell."

"I'm looking for Beck Chandler."

He snorted, "Yeah, I figured. Beck's quite popular these days. Except he's not here."

Benjy saw me gently wave my hand in front of my face to fan away some of the fumes coming from him. He said, "Hey, it's legal here now."

I ignored his remark and said, "When do you think Beck will be back?"

He shrugged, "Hell if I know. Shoved some of his stuff in a duffel bag and took off yesterday afternoon. Hasn't been back since."

"Do you know where he went?"

"Nope. Some guy, looked like he might have been a cop or something, came to talk to him yesterday. After the guy left, Beck looked spooked. Like

I said, he grabbed a few things, and he was gone. Didn't say where he was going."

"You said the man who came to speak to him was a police officer? Did he say why he wanted to talk to Beck?"

Benjy was starting to shift foot to foot, as if he'd had enough of the conversation. "I just said he looked like he *might* be a cop. He wasn't in uniform or anything; he just gave off that vibe. He didn't say why he was here. Beck was in some kind of trouble before, but supposedly he got it all worked out. I thought it had to do with that. Beck was living somewhere else last semester, so I don't know the full story. After Beck left, some other guy came looking for him, too. I told him the same thing I told you. The guy looked pissed off when I told him I had no idea where Beck was, and he left without saying anything else." He looked up and down the street as if he was looking to make sure no one was approaching. "This second guy looked like somebody Beck would be better off not knowing, if you get what I mean."

I figured the first visitor must have been Langley. Whatever information he got from Chandler the first time he spoke to him must have made him think there was reason to question him again. I didn't know why he didn't share the information with Sunny Cody when she asked, other than he wanted to keep her out of the investigation. My impression was that they had a very strained working relationship.

I wondered about the shady appearing guy who came to see Chandler. It sure sounded like it could be somebody who was looking to score some pills. That, added to the fact he had taken off, made Beck Chandler shoot back up the suspect list as far as I was concerned.

After I left Chandler's apartment, I decided to stop by Sunny's house and let her know what I found out from Chandler's roommate. Her mother let me in, and I found Sunny sitting at the dining room table. Her laptop was closed, and a large manila envelope and a combination of typed and written pages were sitting in front of her. She looked immersed in whatever she was reading. When I greeted her, she appeared startled and looked up. "Sorry, I didn't hear you come in. So did you get anything out of Chandler about what's been going on?"

I pulled out a chair and sat next to her. "He wasn't there. His roommate said he took off the other day after someone who 'looked like a cop' came to talk to him. He said Chandler was upset after the cop left. Did Detective Langley tell you he was going to interview him again?"

She threw down the page she had in her hand and said, "He hasn't told me much of anything, only that he's in charge of this case now, and I'm on leave and should let him handle it his way. I reminded him that he asked me to help in the first place, and it is because of that I am on medical leave." She sighed and said, "Did the roommate tell you anything else?"

"Yes, it seems Chandler had another visitor after Langley left. The roommate said another guy came asking for Chandler and was none too happy when he found out he wasn't there."

"Did the roommate say what this guy looked like, or did he get his name or anything?"

I felt a blip of disappointment in myself that I hadn't thought to ask. "No. He just thought the guy looked dangerous."

Sunny sat back and seemed to be staring off into space for a moment. "It seems suspicious he would disappear like that. I don't think we can do much now except wait to see if he resurfaces. I don't think there is enough evidence to charge him with anything yet."

I had another thought, though I didn't want to say it. I hoped something hadn't happened to Chandler. If he was involved with selling narcotics, it was likely he was in contact with some dangerous individuals, and it sounded like his second visitor fit that bill.

I noticed Sunny had her leg propped on a pillow on her chair so her knee was at a forty-five-degree angle. "How's your leg?" I said.

She looked under the table as if to check on it herself. "I'm afraid I didn't do it much good the other day by bearing all my weight on it after that shot was fired. The doctor checked it, though, and she said there didn't appear to be any further damage. However, she said I need to take weight-bearing slow again. How about your ankle?"

I only felt pain if I bumped it against something now. "It's healing well. But I'm afraid I still jump a little at loud noises." I looked at the sheaf of papers in front of her. "Does that have anything to do with our case?" I realized what I had said, but Sunny didn't seem to notice.

She picked up the paper she had been reading and put it back into the envelope and pulled out another page. "I have a good friend who works in the records department. She knew Brian, too. She was devastated when he was killed, and even though she said I was probably going to have to accept the official report of his death eventually, she understood my need to keep digging for more information. They are clearing out some old documents, and she found these buried in another file. These are some of Brian's old notes. They don't appear to be official reports, just notes. She said they must have gotten overlooked when they sent me the rest of his personal papers."

I realized now why she looked like her mind was in another place when I arrived. I know what I felt when I happened upon an old message from my ex, Artie, after he was killed. Artie and I had been divorced for almost two years; I realized how much harder it must be for Sunny. "Isn't it strange? Seeing his writing again, reading what he wrote?"

She cleared her throat, "Yeah. It is."

There was a commotion in the entryway as Sunny's daughter came through the front door and ran to her mother. "Mom! Guess what! Payton got a new puppy! She's so cute! Payton let me hold her, and the puppy licked me. Can we get a puppy?"

Sunny hugged her and said, "Calm down. Did you say hello to Miss Bass.?"

Katie turned to me and said, "Hi, Miss Bass." Then she turned back to her mother, "Can we?"

"I'm not sure about the puppy, honey. Let's talk about that another time. So, you had a fun time over Payton's?" Sunny said.

I stood and said to Sunny, "I'll let you know if I find out anything about where our friend went. Let me know if there is anything else you want me to check on." As I put my jacket on, I said to Katie, "Puppies are so much fun! I bet if you promise to help take care of it, your mom will let you get one." I couldn't hear all of what Sunny was yelling to me as I left, but "Thanks a lot!" was part of it.

Chapter Twenty-Six

I had been so flustered the other day when Justin saw Bruno for his yearly physical that I forgot I needed a refill on his heartworm and flea medication. I figured I would just swing by the veterinarian's office after work the following day and pick up what I needed. When I arrived the waiting room was empty, but there was a commotion going on near the front desk. There were cans and bags of dog and cat food scattered on the floor in front of the shelves that usually held them. One of the higher metal shelves was hanging down. A vet tech came flying out of the back and said to the receptionist, Traci, "He still says no!" She then went over to the mess on the floor and started gathering up the cans and stacking them on the remaining shelves and leaning the bags of food against the wall.

Traci was standing with the phone receiver in her hand but then slammed it down.

"Hi Traci, what happened here? Is there a problem?"

"Yes." The receptionist looked toward the back of the office where the exam rooms were. "Thank heavens we don't have any more appointments booked for today. Dr. McKenzie was taking down a case of prescription dog food for me, and the shelf broke and swung down and hit him on the forehead. Then the box broke open, and a couple of cans hit him on the head, followed by two more of the dog food cases. He's in back, bleeding from a nasty cut on his forehead. We think he needs stitches. One of our vet techs is with him trying to get him to agree to get his injuries checked out, but he is being stubborn and won't go to the emergency room."

Despite how things had been between us lately, and even though he might not listen to me now, I couldn't just let him stand there and bleed. "Would you like me to try to get him to get his injuries checked out?"

Traci looked relieved. "Yes, please."

Justin was in one of the exam rooms, sitting on a stool with a gauze pad pressed to his forehead. The gauze was starting to soak through with blood, and I noticed a small pile of saturated gauze on the counter. It was hard to read his expression when he saw me. It looked like a combination of mortification and relief.

Shauna, one of the practice's vet techs, was standing by the counter removing more gauze from the drawer. She shook her head at me and said, "Maybe you can talk to him."

"I heard you had an accident. Let me see." I reached for the gauze over the wound. He took a few seconds to let me lift it, but he finally gave in. "Have you cleaned it out already?"

"Yes, of course. It's going to be fine. You know how head wounds bleed," he said.

I noticed he wasn't looking at me when he spoke. "It's a pretty good gash; the corner of the shelf must have hit you hard. I do think you need stitches. Plus, I heard you got hit with a couple of heavy cases. How does your head feel? Are you dizzy?"

He just ignored my questions. "I don't want to go to the ED. I'll just put pressure on it a little longer." This time he did look up at me.

"I seem to remember you pushing me to get my head wound checked out when I was injured last summer." I hoped that my pant leg was still covering the healing cut above my ankle bone.

"And I remember you refused to go," he said. I thought I detected the hint of a smile.

What he said was true. "You're just being stubborn. If an animal came in with a laceration like this, you would insist on suturing it, wouldn't you? Plus, you're getting some very impressive contusions on your forehead, and I think you better get your head checked out." I ignored the chuckle that came from Shauna. I placed some more gauze squares over his wound and secured them with a piece of tape. "Come on. I'll drive you."

"I'm sure Shauna can take me." He looked to his vet tech who had been watching this exchange with interest.

Shauna looked at me, "If you're sure you don't mind taking him, that would be great. I would, but I need to pick up my son from daycare." She grimaced at Justin apologetically, "I'm sorry."

Justin sighed and without another word, went to his office to get his jacket and then followed me to my car.

As I climbed behind the wheel, I had a brief thought that maybe I shouldn't have been so quick to offer to drive Justin. It could turn out to be a very uncomfortable ride. I got over my own discomfort by fixating on the situation at hand: Justin needed help, I was able to give it, so it made sense for me to get involved.

It was only a ten-minute drive to the Emergency Department. We drove in silence, but I kept taking quick peeks at Justin to make sure he was still okay. I realized he was also glancing at me periodically. When we turned into the driveway of the medical center, Justin suddenly said, "Do you know how embarrassing this is?"

"Why would you be embarrassed? People have all kinds of accidents, getting beaned with a metal shelf is not that weird, or even that uncommon."

"Not that part of it." He motioned to both of us. "This. I feel embarrassed you had to drive me here."

"Why? You came to *my* rescue in the past. It's the least I can do." I looked at him, and it seemed he was about to say something else, but I cut in, "Whatever happened between…."

I never got a chance to finish. As soon as the car came to a stop, he bolted from the car toward the ED entrance.

"Wait! Don't you want me to come in? How will you get back to your car?"

He yelled over his shoulder, "I'll call an Uber."

I got all the way home before I realized I never picked up Bruno's heartworm medicine. I felt very confused by what had happened with Justin. For a few minutes, while I was checking his wound, it seemed like we had both gotten back to acting as we had when we were together. I knew that my discomfort with him stemmed from the fact that I still had feelings for Justin.

But he seemed uncomfortable too, and it didn't seem like it was because he didn't want to be with me.

As usual, Bruno helped me clear my head. He was always glad to see me and never failed to show it. Before I fed him, Bruno and I went outside to watch the sunset. We went across the road to stand by the tidal marsh where the sea grass had turned yellow, and the water was just a few dark patches interrupting it. The sky was pink with hints of orange, and it was hard to stand there and not be overwhelmed by how beautiful it was. I let my mind drift and forgot about how things were with Justin, the fact that Beck Chandler had disappeared, and someone had fired a shot that came uncomfortably close to hitting me.

I took Bruno into the backyard to play a quick game of fetch. The sun finished setting, and it had gotten too dark to see when Bruno and I went back into the house. I left my cell phone on the counter when I went outside, and when I checked it after I came back in, I saw that I had missed a call from Lynn. I waited until after I had dinner to call her back. I hadn't spoken to her since our dinner with Alex, and I knew she would want to talk about it.

She was her usual upbeat self when I called her back. "So. What did you think of Alex? I know he really liked you. He told me I was lucky to have made such a good friend so quickly."

That statement made me want to be even more tactful with my opinion. "He seemed nice. He is as handsome as you said he was. I guess I never got a chance to notice that before when I was at High Life Dermatology. And I could certainly see that you two are in love." I struggled to find at least one more positive thing to say about him before I hit her with my concerns. She was way ahead of me, however.

Her voice was wary. "But…? I can tell you have something else you want to say."

"I think he was a little cavalier about your safety." I let it out all in one breath. "I mean, he didn't seem all that concerned when you mentioned that your mail had been tampered with, and I'm sure you've told him about the guy watching you and even following you. He didn't even seem to think the two were connected."

It was a few seconds before she answered, and I was afraid I had upset her. "He may have acted that way because I guess I've underplayed what is going on. I didn't tell him about the guy following me on my walks, and when I mentioned that I thought he was watching me, I admitted I might just be acting paranoid. It could be a coincidence that the guy is outside at the same time as me, or maybe he watches everyone in the complex." Her voice became brighter again. "Besides, I've been spending most of my nights at Alex's now, so it isn't really an issue."

It was me who was upset now. "Lynn, you were not being silly or paranoid. And when you told me about him, you were really freaked out! Why wouldn't you share everything that is happening with Alex, a man who you plan to marry?"

"I don't know, okay?" I could tell she was angry, but then she took a breath and said, "I know I should, and I do tell him everything else, but I find this hard to talk about with him."

I suddenly thought of Justin and where sharing everything we did and felt had gotten us. As if she could read my mind, she asked, "You still haven't heard from Justin, have you?"

"As a matter of fact, I saw him when I took Bruno for a checkup." I proceeded to tell her about the visit to the vet and how awkward it had been. Since I was still trying to process what had happened with him that afternoon, I didn't mention it to her.

"Hmmm. Do you think that Justin arranged to be the one to see Bruno that day?"

I hadn't even thought of that. "No. Kerri, one of the receptionists, said Dr. Reddy was sick that day, so Justin just stepped in." I suddenly wanted to change the subject. "Things got a bit interesting the other day in the case I am helping Detective Cody with. I was shot at."

She gasped. "What?!"

"I don't think whoever fired the shot actually meant to hit me, but I got a flesh wound when a flowerpot broke." I went on to tell her about the vandalism of a parent's car and a little bit about questioning some of the kids who might be involved in that and that we had one suspect regarding the drug incident, but that he had disappeared. Since I knew Detective Cody wouldn't approve, I was careful not to mention any names. I only told her enough to give her an idea of what had been going on with the investigation.

"Holy crap! Do I have to be worried now?"

"Detective Cody made me promise if it got any more dangerous, I would back off from the investigation." However, most people would call being shot at being pretty dangerous.

"Were your fingers crossed behind your back when you promised?"

I laughed. "No comment."

"I called you for another reason, besides to find out what you thought about Alex. I was wondering if you would have time later this week to come here and help me look online at some bridal gowns. I plan to go in person to try them on, but I want to get an idea of what's out there before we go. I'll make lunch for us when you come."

I found myself excited at the prospect of helping her look. "Sure, I'd love to. Are we still looking at a spring wedding?"

"Yes. I'm standing firm on that."

I was glad to hear that. "Good. I'll bring Bruno too. I know he'd love to spend some time with you."

It was hard to resist being swept up in Lynn's excitement over her impending wedding. But when we ended our call, I still felt like I had some qualms about Alex. I realized I had only spent a few hours with him, and maybe I'd misinterpreted his reaction to the possibility of Lynn having a stalker. Especially now since I knew she hadn't been completely honest with him about what was going on. Perhaps he would react differently once he knew the whole story.

Chapter Twenty-Seven

The first two patients on my list of visits for the next day were follow-up visits and went well. When I looked at my schedule to see who my first patient of the afternoon was, however, I thought Judy, my supervisor, had made a mistake.

"Judy, I see I have a visit scheduled to see Charlie Duggan. Did something happen to him? I spoke to him a few days ago, and he was fine." I felt a moment of panic. Why hadn't Charlie called me if he had a problem or felt unwell?

Judy sighed and shook her head, "The biggest problem he has is still his insufferable orneriness. Dr. Moore saw him yesterday and was a bit concerned about his blood pressure. Mr. Duggan said he didn't want to be on meds for hypertension. He was quite firm about that, and Dr. Moore made a deal with him that if he let someone come in to check his blood pressure and it was back to his normal, he could hold off on the medication."

I was well acquainted with Charlie's tendency to dig in his heels when he didn't want to do something. "I'm guessing his physician didn't feel confident he would do it himself and then report back what his readings were."

"Yes. And you are the only one who has a good enough relationship with him to get him to cooperate with his care. I sent our new health aide, Kendra, to do his diabetic foot care last week and he insisted that his insurance only be charged half for the visit since he only had one foot. I'm pretty sure he was just joking, but the poor girl didn't know what to do. She asked me to never schedule her to see him again."

I felt bad for Kendra, but it was kind of funny.

As soon as he let me in, Charlie said, "I'm fine, so you don't have to go fussing."

"That's not what I heard," I said. "Dr. Moore is only trying to do what's best for you, if he thinks you need medication to keep your blood pressure under control, then you should trust him."

"Told you, I'm fine."

Charlie held out his arm for me to take his blood pressure, though he didn't look at me while I checked it. I was happy to see that it was normal.

"It's good now. I'll let Dr. Moore know, but I think he's going to want you to check it every day for a while. Do you need me to get a machine for you?"

"No. I have one." He motioned toward his bedroom. He must have seen the confusion on my face. "When my wife was alive, she used to have to take her blood pressure. I still have one of those things in the closet somewhere."

"You need to report back to the doctor what your readings are too. Are you going to do that?"

He glared at me. "Why would I go through the bother of doing it if I wasn't going to let him know? Don't know what was going on the other day, but as you can see, I'm over it now."

I had a guilty thought. "I hope my sharing with you what is going on in the investigation with Detective Cody isn't upsetting you."

"No!" He said it so loud, his ancient Pomeranian, Rex, popped up from the chair he had been sleeping in and looked around for where the disturbance was coming from. "Being involved in the real thing is a lot better than just reading about solving crimes." He motioned to the stack of thrillers and mystery novels on a side table.

I was worried that he'd gotten himself so worked up his blood pressure was going to be elevated again.

He cleared his throat and said, "I talked to Ralph at the garage where I take my car, and he said he didn't have any record of a car like we described with front-end damage. He said the cops came around asking the same thing. He's a good guy. I believe what he says. My friend that owns the body shop is visiting his daughter in California and won't be back for a couple of days. I tried to get the information out of the son-in-law who took over the business, but he wouldn't talk to me. Says he doesn't know me from Adam and he isn't gonna discuss anything about his clients with me."

I realized it was unlikely we'd be any more successful than the police in asking around about the car, though it was worth a try. "Thanks for checking, Charlie." My ankle, where my wound was healing, itched, and I reached down to scratch it.

Charlie motioned to my leg, "What happened there?"

I recounted to him what happened when Detective Cody and I questioned Nick Meyers and his mother, the bullet that hit so close to me, and Beck Chandler's disappearance.

When I was finished, he leaned back hard into his chair and said, "You've been holding out on me! That's a lot going on." There was no mistaking the look of excitement on his face. "So, what's our next move? You're still going to follow up on the information you got, aren't you?" He paused, then said, "I suppose I can't blame you if you don't want to, though."

"No, I want to see this through. I'm pretty sure Nick's mother knows he was lying about where he got the drugs, but I could have sworn he was telling the truth about Chandler not being the one who gave them to him. Though now it certainly looks suspicious that Chandler took off, and no one seems to know where he went. Especially since it sounds like Detective Langley went to question him again before he disappeared. He must still have suspicions about Chandler too."

Charlie looked like he was thinking. "There were two cars when you were with Cody that day, right? And there was supposed to be a drug sale that day. The guy who was killed, Bourne, didn't tell the cops who was going to be there?"

"Detective Cody said he had supplied the name of two of the men who were supposed to be there to make the deal but didn't know who the third was. The guy who was in the car with Bourne took off, and the police haven't been able to find him since. It also turned out that one of the men who Bourne said would be in the car making the delivery could not have been there that day. He was in the hospital in Bridgeport after becoming the victim of a knife attack. The police don't have any information on who replaced him."

"Seems like any information this Bourne guy had was wrong and wasn't going to do the police much good anyway. So why was he killed? Maybe somebody thought he knew more than he did." Charlie said.

That made sense. I thought of what Detective Cody said about Bourne telling her he had information that might interest her personally. But he had been wrong about who was going to be making the delivery on Windy Reed Road that day, so how valuable was any of his information? It was also possible he was bluffing about what he knew to start with.

"I'm not sure how Beck Chandler fits into this, though," I said. "I don't see him as being someone who would be involved in the rough end of the drug trade."

"Hmm," Charlie said, "you'd be surprised."

That reminded me of what his roommate had said about the shady-seeming guy coming to look for Chandler.

I suddenly realized what time it was and that I had to hurry unless I wanted to be late for my next appointment. "I need to leave, but I promise I'll let you know if I find out anything else. Give me a call if you have any more thoughts on the matter, or if you learn anything from your friend when he gets back." I got up to leave, "I'm trusting you to do as you promised and monitor your blood pressure and report it back to Dr. Moore's office."

He made a sour face, but said, "Yeah, yeah. I will."

I let myself out.

I didn't have to go far to see my next patient. It was Charlie's neighbor, Emma Reynolds. I was scheduled to do a set of vital signs, check her oxygen with an oximeter, and her general wellness. She had been to see her physician for a complaint of cough and shortness of breath. A Covid test proved negative, but her doctor was concerned that she could be developing pneumonia. Since she lived alone, he wanted her admitted to the hospital for observation. She refused despite his best efforts to convince her it was the best plan. Dr. Wharton had reluctantly agreed to send her home on antibiotics, with a scheduled visit today by my agency and a stern warning to call 911 if she felt worse. I wondered if there was something in the water on West Street that caused all the senior residents there to be so obstinate.

When I rang the bell, I didn't get any response for several minutes. I was beginning to think I should call 911 myself when Mrs. Reynolds answered the door. She looked a little pale and coughed a few times into a tissue she held to her mouth, but otherwise didn't seem too ill.

"Hi, Mrs. Reynolds. Remember me? I'm from Coretrack Home Health. I came to check on you and see how you're feeling."

She looked apologetically at me. "Oh, dear. I do remember you. I'm so sorry. I'm feeling much better today, and I called to cancel the appointment. I guess your agency didn't let you know."

No, they hadn't let me know, and even if she had tried to cancel, I don't think her doctor would have let her. "Oh, well, I'm here now. Why don't I just take a quick listen and check your oxygen levels?" I nudged a bit closer to her so she would have to step back from the doorway. "It won't take long." I gave her my brightest smile.

She hesitated a few moments longer, and I think she would have tried to close the door if I wasn't already halfway into the house. She seemed annoyed, but said, "All right. If it won't take long. I still do need to rest, you know."

She shuffled into her living room and perched on the edge of the cushion in one of her armchairs. The last time I had been to see her, she had a cast on her left forearm. I was pleased to see that she had graduated to an arm brace.

I took out my stethoscope and oximeter. "I'm so glad to hear you're feeling better today. Dr. Wharton was quite worried about you."

She nodded as I listened to her chest. "Antibiotics are really starting to work, I think."

She had one coughing spell while I listened, and her breath sounds were still slightly coarse, but her oxygen level was good. She did seem to be doing better, or at least seemed to be avoiding the need to be hospitalized. "I'll let Dr. Wharton know that you're recovering well."

I heard a muffled thump coming from down the hallway, and then her large ginger cat skittered into the room.

She leapt up off her chair and said, "I really want to thank you for checking on me, but like I said, I think I need a nap now." She scooped up the cat and headed toward the door, obviously expecting me to follow.

"Do you have any other concerns or questions for me before I go?"

She gave me a strained smile and shook her head, "No. Nothing I can think of."

I was suddenly ahead of schedule, having just made one of the quickest visits of my day.

When I got home that evening, there was a small pot of African Violets sitting by my front door. I picked them up and saw an envelope taped to the side. I set the pot on the kitchen table and waited until I had greeted and fed Bruno before I opened the envelope to see who had left it. The card inside said, *"Thank you for being willing to help the other day."* It was signed *"J."*

I stood for a moment, unsure how I felt. I was annoyed that there was any question about me helping Justin, how could he think otherwise. But I also was a bit touched by the gesture of leaving me a small present to thank me. I tried not to read too much into it. Just thinking about our recent interactions left me feeling a little unbalanced. Was he having thoughts about trying to resume our relationship? I was confused how I felt about that. I was too exhausted now to dwell on it and decided that for now I would just wait and see what happened.

Chapter Twenty-Eight

Lynn called me the next day to remind me she wanted me to come over for lunch and a session searching the internet for ideas about bridal gowns. I loaded Bruno into the car and we headed to see "Auntie Lynn."

I was delighted at how elaborately some of the houses were already decorated for Halloween. As Bruno and I drove to Lynn's condo in North Guilford, we passed yards where bushes were laced with spider webs and handkerchief ghosts hung from tree branches. There were several with jack-o-lanterns already lined up on front steps, as well as houses where orange lights outlined the fronts as precursors to the colored lights that would replace them after Halloween. My favorite, however, was the house we passed where three skeletons dressed in flannel shirts and winter hats sat around a make-believe campfire, roasting marshmallows on sticks. All this reminded me that it was less than two weeks until Halloween, and I had not thought to do any sort of decorating on my own house. "I better at least get a pumpkin so I can carve a Jack-O-Lantern." I said to Bruno. He looked at me and wagged his tail at the sound of my voice.

As I drove toward the end of the complex where Lynn's condo was located, it didn't look like many people were out and about. I was particularly looking to see if there were any men lurking around who fit the description Lynn had given me of her stalker. There was no one I could see.

As usual, Lynn was eager to give Bruno a good petting and belly rub as soon as we entered her place.

"Thanks for coming, Melanie. I figure we can look at some dresses online so I can get an idea of what I want before I go into a shop to pick one out." She took both my hands in hers and said, "Tell me the truth. Do you think it's silly that I want a real bridal gown and the whole rigmarole for this wedding?" She dropped my hands as she said, "It's just that I never did that with Artie or Doug. Like I told you, Artie and I just went to a JP, and Doug thought that we should have a very low-key ceremony. At his suggestion, I just wore a simple light blue dress, and he wore khakis and a short-sleeved shirt. I should have seen the future of our marriage in how unenthusiastic Doug was over the whole ceremony."

"I think you deserve to have the wedding you want. You will look beautiful in any wedding gown you choose." I noticed her eyes filled a little when I said that, and mine did too, because I really believed what I said.

She gave me a quick hug and then said, "I made a chicken salad for lunch, and then we can see if I can find my dream wedding dress." Before we sat down to eat, she went to a small container on her counter and pulled out a dog biscuit. Handing it to Bruno, she said, "I haven't forgotten about you."

The number of wedding dresses we found online was overwhelming at first, but then it became easy to weed out a lot of choices. Some were outrageous (to us anyway): see-through dresses with strategically placed white fabric, severely fitted mermaid gowns with fur-trimmed hemlines—Lynn said she would surely topple over trying to walk in one of those, and micro mini creations that were just—no. Another batch was gorgeous, but waaay beyond what Lynn felt was reasonable to spend on a wedding gown. We bookmarked several that were serious contenders and decided to take a break.

Lynn got up to make tea and cut the apple cinnamon bread she had made. "You will go with me when I go to try on bridal gowns, won't you?"

"Of course. I think that is in the maid of honor guidebook, isn't it?"

"Great. And we need to find a dress for you also. Is there any particular color you would object to?"

I started to reply, but then Bruno suddenly picked up his head from where it was lying by my feet and started to growl. He was staring at the window opposite where I was sitting. I caught a quick glimpse of movement, like someone had been looking in, and had just ducked out of sight. Bruno jumped up and started to bark frantically.

Without saying anything, I leapt up and rushed to the front door with Bruno and Lynn right behind me. I picked up Bruno so he wouldn't run out of the door and stepped out to look around.

"What is it?" Lynn asked.

"I think someone was watching us from your kitchen window," I said. I began to walk around the side of the building. I didn't see anybody, but Bruno suddenly started to squirm and jumped down, barking and chasing something, or someone. I ran after Bruno, following his barks which had now turned back to growls.

Bruno was latched onto the pant leg of a man who was trying to get to the wooded area behind Lynn's condo unit. The guy was trying to shoo him back and kept shaking his pant leg to get Bruno off.

"Stop! What are you doing?" I yelled to the man as I approached him. Lynn came up behind me.

"That's him! That's the guy that has been stalking me!"

"Call your dog off!" The guy hollered.

"Come, Bruno. Good boy," I said, then turned to Lynn. "Call the police!"

Bruno growled one more time, then let go of the man's leg and came as instructed. I scooped him up, but he continued to growl at the man as I held him.

Lynn had thought to grab her phone as she ran out of the house after me, and she held it ready to dial 911.

The man began to walk toward us slowly, his hands raised in a surrender position. "No! Don't call the cops. I can explain." We began to back up as he approached us, and he stopped several feet away.

Lynn paused before punching in 911 and said, "What were you doing looking in my window? And why have you been following me and watching me, you pervert?!"

He smiled, "I've been called lots of worse things. I'm sorry if I frightened you." He looked from one of us to the other.

"So, explain," I said, putting Bruno down again, but giving him the command to stay.

"It's my job. I was hired to investigate you." He tipped his chin toward Lynn, then slowly reached into his shirt pocket and pulled out a business card. I grabbed it from his hand.

It said "Robert Ames—private investigations" and gave his contact information. I handed the card to Lynn.

He motioned to Lynn, "I have to say you've turned out to be pretty boring."

She took a step toward him. "What do you mean?"

"Sorry, no offense. I just meant there were no crimes, no other boyfriends, no sex scandals, no history of bilking rich dudes for their money. That kind of thing."

"I meant, what do you mean you were hired to investigate me? Who hired you?" Lynn asked.

He put his hands up again, "I can't tell you. I must be losing my touch; you were never supposed to find out about any of it. Look, I'll tell my client you're on the level. So, no harm done."

I was getting angry now, and by the look on Lynn's face, she was close to committing assault. "Who hired you?" I grabbed the phone from Lynn's hand and held it up. "I have a friend who is a cop."

"Don't. Okay. It was a woman who said she was interested in protecting her family. Her name is Drover."

I dropped the phone in shock. I couldn't begin to guess how Lynn felt.

Lynn's voice was icy, "First name. What is her first name?"

Mr. Ames took a moment to reply, "Diana, I think."

"Alex's mother?"

I looked quickly at Lynn to make sure she was still all right. She was frozen in place, breathing rapidly.

"I think you better leave now," I said to Mr. Ames, then I picked up Lynn's phone off the ground and took her by the arm to lead her toward her condo. I called Bruno to follow us and shouted over my shoulder to the PI, "Don't come anywhere near her again!"

When we got back into the house, Lynn burst into tears. I went to hug her.

"I'm just so angry! I told you there was something about that woman that wasn't right. How can I deal with having her as a mother-in-law!?" She started to pace back in forth in the kitchen, and I realized she needed to work off some of her rage. "How could she think that I was after Alex's money? That's so insulting! And she is so underhanded. How could she have hired someone to watch me like that, to invade my privacy!"

She finally collapsed into one of the kitchen chairs, and I got her a drink of water. Bruno, bless him, immediately came to put both paws on her knees, and she picked him up to cuddle him.

"What should I do now? Should I tell Alex what his mother did?" She looked up at me expectantly.

I didn't want to bring up the question of whether Alex already knew about what his mother was doing. She would come to that question herself soon enough, I thought. I sincerely hoped he didn't and that he would be as incensed that his mother had Lynn investigated as she was.

"I think you have to talk about this with Alex, but maybe it would be better if you let the shock and anger wear off a little first," I said.

She shook her head and said, "I don't know. That could take a while."

"Why don't I fix us another cup of tea, though I know something stronger might be in order." Lynn gave me a shaky smile, then stared down at the tabletop as if she was deep in thought.

I put the kettle on and rummaged around to find the tea and rinsed out the cups and spoons we had used for our first cup of tea. Her laptop was still open on the table, and I reached to shut it down and close it. "Maybe we should finish looking another day."

Lynn sighed, then said, "I'm pretty sure I would have preferred Mr. Ames turned out to be a stalker rather than what he was." She took a deep breath and looked up at me. "Well, I'm not going to let that woman cause me to end my relationship with Alex. That is what she wants, obviously."

It was alarming that Alex's mother had now become "that woman." What she had done was horrible, and certainly insulting to Lynn, but if Alex and Lynn were to have any kind of marriage, I believed Lynn was going to have to find a way to forgive her.

I tried to put a more positive spin on the situation, though I think I would have been just as upset as she was had I been in Lynn's shoes. "Maybe she was just trying to look out for Alex's best interests. It could be she felt his ex-wife was a gold digger and wanted to protect him from getting hurt again."

The look she gave me made me say, "Okay. I agree. There is no excuse for what she did."

Lynn jumped up and began to pace again. "That's why when I met her, she didn't seem interested in my job or the fact that I was trying to make it as an artist or even was surprised at my past marriages and the fact Artie was murdered last summer. She knew all about me already!" Lynn slammed her fist down on the counter.

I was a bit taken aback as I had never seen her so worked up and so angry. Just then, the kettle started to whistle. "Here, take a deep breath and sit down. I'll pour the tea."

Lynn did as I suggested, but I could still feel the fury radiating off of her. Bruno had retreated to under the table and now sat nestled close to the chair I had been sitting in.

I fixed both our cups of tea and set hers in front of her. She shrugged as if shaking something off. "I'm sorry. I just can't believe Mrs. Drover went to such lengths. I will calm down now, and I will think of a way to handle this."

She seemed to gradually transform back into the calm, even-tempered woman I had come to know. She smiled at me, "Thank you, Melanie, for putting up with my burst of temper."

I took her hand across the table and squeezed it. "Of course. You had every right to be upset. But you're right; you need to think of a way to get past what she did."

Lynn took a sip of her tea and said, "I was sad that Alex was going to be away tonight at a conference in Philadelphia, but now I'm glad. It will give me a little bit of time to think of how to let him know that my stalker was instead snooping on me per orders of his mother."

I thought of how unconcerned Alex seemed when Lynn told us about someone tampering with her mail. I resisted saying anything to Lynn, deciding to wait and see what his reaction was when she told him about Robert Ames.

"Alex said he was going to call me tonight. It's going to be hard to pretend that everything is all right. I do think I need to tell him in person, though."

Now that Lynn had calmed down a bit, Bruno went over to her and put his paws on her knees again and began to lick her hands. She picked him up into her lap. "Here is our hero. You caught that creep so we could find out what he was up to!"

I went over to scratch Bruno behind the ears. "You're right. He alerted us that someone was looking in the window. And he wasn't going to let him get away."

Lynn laughed, "Did you see the look on Ames's face when Bruno had him by the leg of his pants?"

"I know. And the way he yelled at me to call off my dog, you would have thought Bruno was a Rottweiler!" I was glad we could laugh a bit about it now. I cleared our cups from the table and placed them in her sink. "I think Bruno and I need to get home now, but we will get together another day in our search for a dress."

"Yes. I plan on making our wedding a beautiful event, no matter what happens with his mother."

Lynn walked us to the door and said, "I'll let you know what Alex says after I tell him."

I didn't enjoy the ride home nearly as much as I had the ride to Lynn's house. I had to admit I felt relieved that her stalker hadn't turned out to be a physical threat to her after all. But I felt terrible that she now had a big issue to deal with in her relationship with Alex. Whether or not he was close to his mother, she is his mother, and if she and Lynn did not get along, it would make things difficult for everyone. This made me think again of Justin and how our relationship had ended. Or hadn't.

As if to accent the awful end to the afternoon, it had started to rain, and all the cheerful Halloween decorations I had noted on the drive to Lynn's now looked droopy and sad.

Chapter Twenty-Nine

The rain had increased in intensity by the time we got home, and Bruno and I made a run for it to get into the house before we became thoroughly soaked. After I dried him off, Bruno found a comfy spot in a corner of the sofa and settled in for a nap. I was a bit damp myself and decided to change into dry clothes.

As I passed through the kitchen after putting my wet clothes in the washer, I noticed the African Violet Justin had left for me was still sitting on the table. I checked to be sure it didn't need any water and placed it on the kitchen windowsill where it would get indirect sunlight when the sun came out again. It saddened me that now not only was my personal life on the rocks, but there was a blip in Lynn's love life also. I was still incredulous over the fact Alex's mother had hired a Private Investigator to check on Lynn to be sure her intentions were honest.

Lucky for Mrs. Drover that Lynn was really who she appeared to be because it seemed Robert Ames might not be the most competent of investigators. He wasn't very good at keeping his cover for one thing. Lynn quickly noticed him watching and following her, though we thought he had more nefarious intentions than that of a private eye. I wondered how Mrs. Drover would react when Mr. Ames had to inform her his cover was blown, and Lynn was none too happy when she found out what he was up to.

After I was warm and dry again, I decided that since I had nothing else planned for the day, I would make myself one of my favorite dinners. One of the things that I missed about Lynn being my housemate was her fabulous cooking. I know how to cook, and I am rather good at it I think, but when I am just making a meal for myself, I tend to go for quick and simple. This day called for a comforting meal, however. I love Chicken Marsala and checked to see that I had what I needed to make it. I raided the refrigerator and the cupboards only to find I was missing two key ingredients: mushrooms and Marsala wine. I looked out the window to see that the rain had stopped, at least temporarily, and the sun was attempting to come out again.

Bruno picked up his head as I put my jacket on, but I said, "Stay here. I'll be right back." In response, he settled his head back on his paws. I guess his earlier heroics had tired him out.

The rain must have kept some people away, or I hit Stop and Shop at a good time because there didn't seem to be as many people as usual shopping. I was able to breeze up and down the aisles. Even though I'd only gone in for a few items, I found myself thinking of more and more things I was low on, and I loaded up my cart as I thought of things. I'd made it to the end of the tomato sauce and pasta aisle when the sound of voices in the next aisle stopped me just as I was about to turn the corner. The voices were familiar. It sounded like Anna Meyers and Audrey Cullen. I backed up a bit so I wasn't visible, but so I still was able to hear what they were saying. Or at least most of what they were saying. It seemed as if they were trying to keep their voices down.

"I just feel stupid that we stood up for him and for what happened to Beth's car."

"Shhh!" I recognized Anna's voice. "The damage has been taken care of now. She's satisfied, so there'll be no more trouble."

"What do you think happened to make him leave?" It was Audrey's voice. "You don't think he really was dealing drugs?"

Anna was quick to cut her off, "Do you?"

Audrey hesitated a few seconds before answering, "I didn't, but now—I don't know. I heard the police still think he was involved. Then suddenly, he's gone without telling anyone where he was going. I heard Beth Forbes is gloating, saying she was right all along and it was a mistake to let him coach the boys."

Anna said, "I'll admit it does make him look like he's guilty."

I thought it was interesting how she suddenly changed her opinion of how innocent Beck Chandler was. Both women stopped talking for a moment, and I saw another shopper round the corner coming from their aisle. When they resumed their conversation, their voices were lowered even more, so I only caught snatches of what was said.

"...the police! Tyler told me...I don't want my son...Nick's been his best friend forever but...if there is..." Audrey sounded agitated now.

"I would never put...Nick wasn't lying about...won't happen again." Anna sounded a bit on edge.

I could hear Audrey better as she answered, "I know that. But I'm worried. Anna, if there's anything I can do..."

"I'm fine. Thanks."

I was startled by a loud "Excuse me! I need to reach that pasta." I turned to see a young woman with a toddler in the child seat of her cart.

"I'm sorry." I moved out of her way, and by the time she grabbed her rigatoni and continued down the aisle, I could no longer hear the two women talking. It seemed like they had moved on also.

Since I had gotten what I came into the store for, plus some, I decided to pay for my groceries and then wait and see if I could catch Audrey as she left the store. Maybe I could find out what was worrying her about Anna or her son. I waited near my car, where I had a view of both exits from the Stop and Shop. I was also watching to see Anna exit, so I could make sure she didn't see me.

I saw Audrey come out of the store. Thankfully, she was by herself. I had loaded my groceries in the car so I could approach her, pretending to be just entering.

"Hi, Audrey. I thought that was you."

"Hello." Her greeting was curt. She started to walk away, but then turned around again and motioned to me to step aside toward the cart area. "Tyler said you were with the detective who came to question Nick the other day. It was the detective who got injured by the car that day on Windy Reed, wasn't it?"

"Yes. Detective Cody. She wanted to talk to Nick again, and I was driving her." I expected her to ask me why the heck it was me driving her and what right I had to be there.

Instead, she looked uneasy and said, "What did Nick tell the detective? Tyler gave me his version of what Nick and his mother said, but you know how teenagers are."

I wasn't sure what rules of confidentiality applied if you weren't actually a police officer who had interviewed a suspect. "Nick still said he found the pills in the boys' bathroom at the school. He said he found them by accident." I thought she must be worried that Tyler had a part in the incident. "I don't think Tyler had anything to do with Nick getting the pills."

"Of course he didn't! But it sounds like the police don't believe Nick's story. Does your detective friend still suspect Beck Chandler of supplying the drugs to the boys?"

The fact she brought Chandler up seemed to indicate she questioned Nick's explanation, also. "I'm sure you've heard he has disappeared, so I'm afraid that does make him look suspicious," I said.

"I guess it does." She hesitated a moment. "Can I ask you something? How did Nick ...and Anna... seem to you?"

Her question surprised me. "A little nervous, I think. Of course, it could have been because they were being questioned by the police."

She nodded but looked away from me for a moment.

"Why do you ask?" I said.

She sighed and said, "Nick and Tyler have been best friends since kindergarten. Nick has spent a lot of time at our house and Tyler at his. But lately, Tyler is over at Nick's house most of the time despite the fact I encouraged him to have Nick come to ours. He says it's because Nick has a better video game system than he does."

"And that bothers you?" I asked.

She paused, then continued, "Anna and Joe, Nick's parents, split two years ago. I don't know exactly what happened. Anna said Joe had an affair with someone in his office, but I've also heard different stories. I never pressed her for the details. Anyway, Anna seemed to be coping okay with the divorce, and I guess having the boys over kept her company. But lately, something seems—off—with her." Audrey looked a little embarrassed now. "This fall, she was spending a lot of time hanging around and talking to Beck Chandler. At first, I suspected they might be seeing each other on the sly, and she was embarrassed because he was the boys' coach and much younger than her. But now I don't know. Lately, it seems like something else is going on."

Audrey had picked up on some kind of undercurrent with Anna Meyers also. "How about Nick? How does he seem to you?"

"Like I said, I don't see as much of him as I used to, but he does seem more stressed than usual. Maybe that's why he took the pills. Tyler swears Nick hasn't used drugs again since that day, but maybe he just hasn't seen him do it." Her demeanor suddenly changed, "Look, I don't know why I told you all this." She started to walk away but stopped and turned around again. "You're a nurse. You would know if someone was going to hurt themselves, right?"

Her question sent up a red flag for me. I nodded and said, "Some things to look for are mood changes, hopelessness, or stress. Drug use. Who are you worried may be..."

She suddenly bolted away toward her car before I could finish my question. But now I was worried also, wondering who she was afraid would harm themselves.

I did make Chicken Marsala for dinner, but I found I didn't enjoy it as much as I had anticipated.

Chapter Thirty

I mulled over the events of the previous day as I ate my yogurt and fruit for breakfast. There was nothing I could do to help Lynn except to listen to and support her when she told Alex about the private eye his mother hired. I wasn't sure who Audrey was worried about. I didn't think it was her son, Tyler. However, she did seem a bit concerned that he spent so much more time at his friend's than at home. She had mentioned Nick being upset lately. I wondered if Tyler had told her anything about him that made her think Nick was in even more trouble than we knew about and that Tyler was worried he might harm himself. Nick had turned to drugs, at least once anyway, and that often was a sign of depression. He certainly seemed to be hiding something when Sunny questioned him. Keeping a secret could certainly create a heavy burden. Although Anna had refused Audrey's offer of help, I hoped she'd get help somewhere if she thought Nick was in danger.

Audrey's suspicion that Anna might have been having an affair with Beck Chandler was an interesting thought. That would explain Anna defending him when he was accused of providing the drugs to the boys and in the vandalism on Beth Forbes's car. Except she seemed to have changed her tune when she spoke to Audrey yesterday. I wonder if she felt rejected when he disappeared suddenly.

A single bark by my side interrupted my thoughts. "Okay, I know. Let's go for a quick walk before I leave for work."

That evening after work, as I pulled closer to my house, I saw there was a car parked in front. A car I recognized. Justin was sitting on my front stoop. My heart rate suddenly picked up. Why was he here? Did he come to say he wanted his plant back, and I was to stay out of his life?

I got out of my car slowly, not sure if I should smile and say hello or let him speak first. He stood up as soon as I approached him, a tentative smile on his face.

"I'm sorry if this isn't a good time," he said. "I...wanted to talk to you."

I was still unsure where this was going. "Sure. Let's talk inside."

The first few minutes were taken up with Bruno greeting both of us, his whole-body wagging, as if he couldn't believe his good luck that both of us were there.

"Excuse me while I put my work things away," I said. This gave me a minute or two to decide how to act next. When I came out of my room Justin was seated in one of the living room chairs, Bruno at his feet. He went to stand, but I motioned for him to stay seated.

I broke the silence first, "So, how is your head healing? Let me see."

He lifted a lock of his hair that had fallen over his wound. "It's fine. It was just a scratch."

I saw he had four stitches in his forehead and a pattern of yellow and green where his bruising was resolving. "Thank you for the plant. You didn't have to."

"Yes. I did." He hesitated, then said, "How are you?"

I realized he was looking directly at my right ankle. I used my left foot to nudge my pant leg further down.

"You don't have to hide it. My grandfather told me what happened. He said to tell you he's sorry, but he's changed his mind about keeping his nose out of our personal business."

I raised the hem of my pant leg now to show him the scabbed over cut. "See, it was really just a scratch."

He laughed, but then let out a deep breath. "My grandfather said someone took a random shot at you. That must have been frightening."

I let the fact that it probably wasn't random slide. "At the time, I was more startled than afraid, and I was glad Detective Cody reacted so quickly. I did feel a little shaky at first, but then afterward, I was more angry than scared. I don't think the person was aiming at me, but it still was a dangerous thing to do." I wondered just how much Charlie had told Justin about what was going on with the investigation.

"I'm very glad that you weren't injured more seriously in that incident, and it makes me nervous to think of what other situations you might get into."

I was afraid we were going to get into another argument, or that he was going to try to make me feel guilty for causing him to worry.

Instead, he said, "I knew as soon as we met that you were a stubb... determined young woman, and also very brave. Those were two characteristics that first attracted me to you." He stopped to take another deep breath. "So, I shouldn't complain when you are acting that way now."

I started to get up to go over to him, but he held out his hand to stop me. "No. Let me finish. I spoke to a friend of mine from school who *did* become a psychologist, and she convinced me that I had to think about why I felt so protective of you. We also discussed the difference between being protective and being smothering. More importantly, I spoke to a cranky old man who is a mutual acquaintance of ours, and he said he hoped he didn't have to smack me with a two-by-four to get me to come to my senses. He said I should explain why I was so fearful for you."

I hid a smile at the thought of Charlie laying down the law to Justin, and I forgave him for going back on his promise not to meddle. I was also anxious to hear Justin's explanation. "Should I make us some coffee and tea?"

"No. Let me get this out first." He rubbed his hands together a couple of times as though thinking of how to start. "I had a close friend in veterinary school. Actually - we were more than close friends, and I began to suspect she might be the 'the one.' We were part of a group who studied together and went out a lot together. One of the guys in our group, Marty, was having a tough time getting the material, though, and was close to flunking out. He got mixed up with some people who promised they could get him 'a little something' to pep him up and help him focus." Justin was watching my face to see if I followed where this was heading.

I nodded for him to continue.

"Anyway, where this guy met his suppliers was not in the best part of town. Amy was the mother hen in our group. She found out what Marty was doing and decided she should follow him and try to dissuade him from going, convince him that it wasn't safe. I only know what happened then from what Marty told us and what the police reported afterward. Amy caught up with Marty once he reached the abandoned building where he was supposed to meet the guy selling him the pills. It turned out the guy supplying the uppers had just had a big fight with his girlfriend over whether or not he was cheating on her. The girlfriend walked in on the trio, assumed Amy was the whore her man was cheating with, and shot both the guy and Amy." He looked at me then. "I felt partially responsible for what happened. I always thought I should have tried harder to stop her from following Marty or at least have gone with her. It's taken a long time for me to let myself get close to someone again. I just can't think about something happening to you."

I felt a lump in my throat. I did go over to him this time and sat on the arm of his chair and began to stroke his back. "I'm so sorry you lost your friend. But there is danger everywhere, some just minor and some catastrophic. All any of us can do is take reasonable precaution."

He took my free hand in his. "That's what my psychologist friend pointed out. She made me realize I wasn't keeping you any safer by refusing to be with you. I was only hurting both of us. So, I wonder if you would consider letting me back into your life?"

I pretended I was thinking about it for a moment, but then said, "Are you still going to nag me about my safety?"

He sighed and said, "Yes, I know I will."

"All right. I know I can't change who you are either." I leaned in then to kiss him.

I convinced Justin to stay for dinner. I told him I had leftover Chicken Marsala that would go to waste if he didn't help me eat it. We talked about mundane things going on with work while we ate, and we both laughed at his grandfather's determination to make us see we should be together. I filled him in on Lynn's engagement and that the man we thought was stalking her was instead spying on her.

"My guess is that didn't go over well with Lynn," he said.

"That's putting it mildly. I'm going to be her maid of honor, and I hope you'll agree to be my plus one. That is, if there is still going to be a wedding. That will depend on what happens when she sees how Alex reacts to the news of what his mother did."

"Tell me where and when, and I'll be there."

Despite the apparent ease of our conversation, I felt there was still a hint of nervousness between us, almost like when we first started dating.

After dinner, Justin said he really had to get home to feed his dog Jasper, and Miss Scarlett, his cat. I walked him to the door, and he hesitated for a moment, then said, "Please don't take this the wrong way, but maybe we should take things slowly for a while."

I had been thinking the same thing. I felt our relationship was still a bit fragile, and I wanted to be sure that this time we stayed cued into each other's feelings. "I like the idea of starting over."

After he left, I couldn't help but feel optimistic, even though I knew we still could have some rocky areas we had to get past.

Chapter Thirty-One

After Justin left, I called Sunny Cody. I thought that the possibility that Anna Meyers and Beck Chandler had been seeing each other could be important. I explained to her what I overheard Anna and Audrey saying.

I told her how I had come upon the women in conversation. "Anna never answered Audrey when she asked if she thought Chandler left because he was guilty of providing drugs to the boys, although she later admitted that was possible. Also, I think they were talking about what happened to Beth Forbes's car. Something about it being taken care of already."

"Hunh. I spoke to Jim Webb. He's the one who responded when Mrs. Forbes called in with the complaint. He said that on a hunch, he asked her neighbor if she had a ring camera. It showed three figures exiting a car and heading toward the Forbes's. It was hard to say for sure, he said, but one of them was wearing a pink sweatshirt, and they all looked more like adult females than high school kids. When he went to let Mrs. Forbes know what he found, she told him she wanted to withdraw her complaint. She wouldn't say why but told him the damage was repaired now, and as far as she was concerned, there was no need to pursue it. She said the figures on the video were some friends visiting her, and then suddenly remembered running over something and thinks that must be what damaged her tires."

That surprised me. "That's absurd! What could she have run over? A blade?"

"Maybe you were right when you questioned whether it wasn't Mrs. Meyers who was involved in the vandalism, not her son. According to the recording, if it was her, she wasn't alone either. She wasn't the only one trying to discourage Mrs. Forbes's complaint about Chandler. As far as Mrs. Forbes wanting to withdraw her complaint, peer pressure doesn't always end in high school. Her son still has a few years left to play sports with the sons of the ladies who we presume did it."

"I had a chance to speak to Audrey Cullen once she left the store. She said she wondered if Beck Chandler and Anna had been seeing one another romantically. She said that they were spending a lot of time talking together at games."

"If that is true, then I suppose that would explain why Mrs. Meyers was so upset that Chandler was under suspicion for dealing drugs."

"But if he was the one Nick got the pills from, I can't believe she would continue to defend him," I said.

She didn't respond to that, and I got the feeling she was concentrating on something else. "Sunny? Did you find out something else?"

"No. Sorry. I was just going over those papers my friend sent me. At first, it didn't look like much new information was in here. A lot of random thoughts Brian scribbled down on various cases he was investigating and even more thoughts on what he wanted to pick up for lunch. The cases are all referred to by number using his own special code. There is no way to know who he was talking about. But I found one scribbled note that refers to meeting a 'Larry.' The meeting was scheduled for the evening he was killed. The official report said Brian came upon an attempted burglary at Price Electronics, and when he tried to stop him, the perpetrator shot him. As I told you before, they tracked down the shooter, but he was dead before they could arrest him. His name was Lawrence Tackman. The official report says Brian surprised him, but it looks like he was supposed to meet him there. I can only assume he thought the guy had some information for him. I don't know why he went alone."

"And you don't know why he would be meeting him?"

"No. I can't find anything in his notes to give me a clue. Anyway, it doesn't look like Brian's death happened exactly as the report said it did. According to the report it was Langley who responded first to the call to

Price Electronics."

"And he was the one who wrote the report, right?"

"Yes. He said everything pointed to it being an interrupted robbery attempt."

"Why would Langley just assume Brian surprised the guy in the midst of a robbery, why wouldn't he investigate further?"

"Because that is what it looked like, on the surface anyway. There was a broken window in the back, and reports of someone seen running across the back parking lot. As I've said before, Langley likes to take the first and most obvious answer he finds."

"No wonder you don't like the guy," I said.

"I never liked him to begin with. This just reinforced the feeling."

I had to agree he seemed pretty lazy in his investigation of who was the source of the drugs making their way into the community. All his efforts seemed to be focused on following up on Beck Chandler. If he was so certain Chandler was involved, why hadn't he found enough evidence to arrest him?

"Has Detective Langley made any progress in finding out who actually was there to make the drug sale on Windy Reed Road?" I asked.

"No. I spoke to him yesterday, and he says with Bourne dead and the information on who would be doing the sale inaccurate, we have hit a wall."

"You do have the name of the guy who was driving the car Bourne was in, though, right? Has he turned up yet?"

"His name is Reno Kemp. No, but I have every confidence he will do something stupid again and get caught. I put in a word at the station that if they get any leads on his whereabouts, I want to be notified too. I reminded them that I have a personal stake in finding who was involved in the incident that day."

Chapter Thirty-Two

The following day I brought Bruno with me as I searched the field at Bishops Farm Market for the perfect Halloween pumpkin. He pranced along at the end of his leash, sniffing each pumpkin I stopped to examine and eagerly greeting all humans and dogs who wanted to say "hello." The day was sunny and crisp and reinforced the sense of contentment I had felt since Justin and I had decided to give our relationship another try.

I had just loaded both Bruno and the pumpkin into the car when I got a text from Lynn: *Cup of tea?*

I quickly replied yes. I couldn't wait to let her know that Justin and I had decided to get back together. Also, she had never called me to let me know how Alex reacted when she told him about the P.I. I figured that was one reason she wanted me to come over. I hoped that he had been at least a little upset and that they had talked about a way to approach his mother with what they knew and set some limits concerning her involvement in their relationship. "Ha!" I thought. "Great advice from someone who is new to figuring out the boundaries in her own relationship!"

As I approached Lynn's place, I saw Robert Ames, the private investigator Mrs. Drover had hired. He was loading boxes into the back of a light gray Honda Civic. I noticed the Red Sox sticker on the back bumper and realized it was his car I had seen speeding away from my house several days ago. At the time, I questioned whether it was the person in a light-colored car that hit Sunny Cody. Lynn had stopped by that evening, and now it looked like it had been Ames following her.

He waved to me as I passed him. I returned his wave with a halfhearted one of my own. Bruno let out a brief "Woof!" and I said, "It's okay, buddy, he was just doing his job."

When I rang her bell, Lynn opened the door, and I noticed she was wearing a fair amount of paint on her arms and clothing. That was not a good sign. When she was upset, she tended to paint quickly with broad strokes, and gobs of paint often didn't make it onto the canvas.

"Hi! Come in." She made a smooching sound toward Bruno and said, "Sorry. I was working on my latest painting, and I got a little carried away. Have a seat while I clean up."

While she was washing up and changing her clothes, I examined the canvas she was working on in a corner of her living room. Despite the way Lynn looked, there was only a small amount of new paint on the drop cloth she used to cover the floor beneath the easel. The painting was gorgeous. She had only just started, but the swirls of blues, greens, and blacks suggested a storm at sea. "Uh Oh!" I thought.

I was startled by a voice behind me. "All right, I can hug you now!" Lynn had come back into the room. She gave me a quick hug and then said hello to Bruno. She looked cheerful, so maybe things had gone well after all.

After we went into the kitchen, I said, "I'm anxious to hear how things went with Alex."

She didn't answer at first, her back to me. She began putting the kettle on and getting down the cups and tea. Finally, she sat opposite me. "Things went well. Sort of." She began to pick some paint she'd missed off her thumbnail. "I told him about Ames, that he was the guy following me and apparently tampering with my mail. I told him that he was hired by his mother to investigate me. Of course, at first, Alex denied it was possible. He insisted his mother would never ever do something like that. He said I must have misunderstood. Then I handed him Ames's business card. I told him Ames claimed he was hired by a woman named Diana Drover. After that, he seemed upset, said he was sorry she did that and that he would certainly speak to her about it."

"That sounds like he will at least confront her about it. That's good." I said.

I could tell by the look on Lynn's face that something was bothering her, though. "What is it?"

"I don't know. Maybe it's nothing, but when I handed him the guy's business card, he hardly looked at it. Like he already knew what it would say."

I had been worried that Alex might not be completely innocent in this situation, and now Lynn had her own suspicions. "What are you thinking?"

"I'm not sure what to think. I don't believe Alex had anything to do with hiring the private investigator to begin with, but maybe he wasn't really surprised that his mother would do something like that." She got up to pour the water for our tea, then said, "I'm worried that Alex may not stand up to his mother and tell her to stay out of our relationship."

"How are things now between you and Alex?"

"I love him, and I don't want to make any rash decisions. He said he would insist his mother apologize, so I will see what happens. For now, I'm not spending any more nights at his house; I'm staying here in my own place. Especially now that I know there is no reason to be afraid I'm being stalked."

"I saw Robert Ames as I was coming in. It looks like he is moving out."

"Yes, my neighbor said he only had a short-term sublet. The owners of the condo he was renting are returning from Europe. I'm glad. Seeing him around the complex is even more awkward now that I know what he was doing."

I felt bad mentioning that Justin and I were back together at a time when there was a problem in her relationship with Alex, but I knew she would be really upset if I didn't tell her right away. "Justin stopped over to my house yesterday."

"What! That's wonderful! It *is* a good thing, right?"

I grinned, "Yes. It was a very good thing." I told her about my taking him to the ER when he got injured. I told her that I thought we both still felt the electricity between us and that he sent me a thank you plant a few days previously.

"He sent you a plant! That's almost as good as flowers. Why didn't you tell me about it right away?!"

"I'm sorry. I just didn't want to get my hopes up that Justin and I could work things out." I realized I hadn't been fair to keep it from her, she had been very open about what was going on with her and Alex. "In any case, when he came over, we talked about it and decided to give our relationship another chance. He told me he blamed himself for the tragic loss of someone he cared about. It happened years ago, but I understand better now why he is so protective and can seem controlling at times. He said in spite of his fears, he realizes he can't change who I am and is trying to accept that." As I explained it to Lynn, I realized that I was asking a lot of Justin, and I needed to be more forgiving and supportive of his efforts to deal with his fears.

"I'm so glad you two worked it out." Lynn looked genuinely pleased for me.

When we went to sit in her living room, I pointed to the painting. "That's beautiful. I love the colors. I was a bit worried, though, when I first saw it. It looks a bit stormy, and I was hoping it didn't reflect your mood."

She laughed, "No. I admit I was a bit unsettled after what happened, but that painting is for a client. You were right. It is of a storm at sea. It's not done, but he wanted a painting of 'a whaling ship weathering a storm' he said. According to him, it's for his home office." She shrugged, "He's paying me very well, so I hope he likes it when it's done."

"That's great you're getting more clients for your painting. Are you still planning to work at High Life Dermatology part-time?" I said.

"No. As a matter of fact, I handed in my resignation two days ago. I felt guilty leaving Alex and the rest of the partners in the lurch, but they said they understood." She smiled again, then said, "From what I heard, they already have someone who has applied for the position. A Mrs. Kirby heard about it from her granddaughter, who is one of our patients. She has thirty years of experience working as a receptionist in a dentist's office and is excited about coming out of retirement to fill the position. I think someone of her age and experience would be an excellent choice!"

Bruno had gone to sit by Lynn's front door, his message that he needed to go out. "I think Bruno and I will let you get back to your painting. I'd love to see it when it's done if there is time before you need to get it to your client."

"I'll let you know when it's finished. And be sure to update me on how things are with you and Justin."

I left feeling better about how things were going in Lynn's life. At least Alex had agreed to speak to his mother about what she did, and I hoped Mrs. Drover would follow through with an apology. I also was glad that Lynn's career as an artist was beginning to take off. My mood improved even more when I got a text from Justin asking if Bruno and I wanted to meet him and Jasper at the bike trail at Hammonasset Beach State Park in an hour.

Chapter Thirty-Three

Bruno got excited as soon as we turned into the entranceway to the park, whining and barking happily. He got even more excited as he spotted Justin and Jasper waiting for us at Meigs Point. The day was sunny and warm for October, but there was a stiff breeze coming off the ocean as we walked from Meigs Point toward West Beach. I wished I had worn a warmer jacket.

After an exchange about how things were going in our work life, Justin cleared his throat and said, "I talked to my grandfather. He said that you have been questioning someone who you think might be involved in dealing drugs, but that he seems to have disappeared now."

"Yes. That's true."

I sensed Justin relax his shoulders a little, "So, things are at a standstill right now. I mean, as far as your involvement is concerned."

I realized he was probably right, and I felt a pinch of disappointment. I didn't know what, or if, there was anything more I could do to help Sunny with the investigation. "I guess you're right. For now." I saw his shoulders tense again. "You don't have to worry. It isn't as if I have been chasing after dangerous criminals, I've only been talking to soccer moms and college kids." I didn't remind him of the shooting incident. "And Detective Cody made me promise if things got more dangerous that I would step away from the investigation."

He stopped and looked at me. "It's not that I don't believe you will try to avoid any real danger, but I'm afraid you may not see it coming until too late."

I took his hand in my free hand and squeezed it, "I promise I will keep my eyes wide open."

He squeezed my hand in return, and we walked on in silence for several minutes.

We walked the mile and a half from Meigs Point to West Beach and then decided to turn around and walked back. On the return trip, I told him what Lynn said about Alex asking his mother to apologize to Lynn for what she had done.

"I'm glad to hear he is standing up to his mother. Although I don't know Alex's mother, I do know Lynn, and I don't see her letting this Mrs. Drover get the best of her," he said.

I had to agree with him.

Justin and Jasper walked me to my car, and after I settled Bruno in, Justin said, "Are you free for dinner Wednesday night?"

"Yes, I am." As I drove away, I found myself already anticipating Wednesday evening.

The week started out on a sour note. On my first appointment of the day, I found ninety-year-old Loretta Jenkins propped on her sofa in her nightgown. She was shaking and tearful. Her left knee was swollen to twice its size, and she complained of a sharp pain in her left hip. She said she had fallen when she got up to use the bathroom but couldn't remember if it was last night or early that morning.

I tried to get her positioned more comfortably on the sofa but every movement caused her more pain. "Did you have your Life Alert monitor on Mrs. Jenkins?" I looked around to see if it was by her side.

"No, it's upstairs. I forgot to put it back on after I changed for bed last evening." I saw her cell phone was on the side table near her. "I didn't want to bother anyone by calling for help. I thought if maybe if I just rested a bit..."

I knew the real reason Mrs. Jenkins did not immediately call for help. She was terrified that if she had to go into the hospital she would never come home again. Unfortunately, there was no question that she would need to be admitted, just as she feared. I was also afraid her dire predictions might prove to be true. It looked as if it was no longer safe for her to live on her own.

I sat down gently next to her and put my hand over hers. "I think we need to call an ambulance and get you taken to be examined."

She took a deep breath and nodded, "All right, if you say so."

I sat with her as we waited for the ambulance to arrive, and I watched her as she looked all around her living room as if committing it to memory.

I called my next patient to let him know I would be a bit late for our appointment, but Mr. Reyes was obviously irritated by that fact, stating that he had other things to do that day besides waiting for me to take my sweet time getting to his house. I hoped that by the time I arrived, he would have cooled down, but his wife shook her head and rolled her eyes as she let me in.

He glared at me as I walked into the living room, where he was reclined on the sofa. "Finally! You medical people think nothing of keeping us regular chumps waiting all day, but heaven forbid I'm ten minutes late getting to an appointment! My appointment gets canceled!"

"I'm sorry, Mr. Reyes. I had an unexpected development at my last appointment." I didn't know where he thought he was going in such a hurry, anyway. He was still dressed in his pajama bottoms and was two days post-op from a rotator cuff repair and couldn't drive.

"Yeah, well, let's get on with it. Do your thing so you can get out of here and torture the next person."

I reminded myself that he was probably in pain, so it might account for his nastiness. But somehow, I doubted pain was the whole cause of his behavior. I was glad to see his wound looked clean and was healing. Despite how he was behaving, he also claimed he was taking his pain meds as ordered and was getting enough relief. So, no excuse there.

I gave his wife a sympathetic look as she let me out. She just shook her head in response.

My last patient of the day lived in a house on a road in a less-developed part of town. As I drove home, I was calmed by the fact there wasn't much traffic on the road, and although the trees were losing a lot of their leaves by now, I still found it a pretty drive. I realized I was not far from the Meyers's house and then couldn't help but think back to what Nick and his mother told Sunny and me when we questioned them. I was still trying to decide how much had been truth, or even if any of it was. What were Nick and Anna hiding and why? Audrey Cullen sensed something was off with either Nick or his mother and was obviously worried about it. Was it because she knew Anna Meyers had been one of the women who had vandalized Beth Forbes's car? I had originally thought when Sunny told me about the Ring video that Audrey had been involved too. Now I wasn't sure that was the case.

I was trying to think of an excuse to approach Audrey and question her about why she was worried about Nick and Anna when a blue Toyota pulled out of a side road without stopping. I shook my head, convinced it was probably a teenager who had given no thought to the fact that there might be other cars on the road. I stayed several car lengths behind the Toyota. If they were driving that crazy, I wanted to be as far away from them as possible. Suddenly the car in front of me began to weave erratically. I hit the horn a long blast in hopes that if they were on their phone, it would remind them to pay attention to the road. The driver straightened the car up for a bit, but then without slowing down at all, suddenly veered off the road, digging up a grassy area at the side of the road, plowing through a heavy patch of brush, and coming to rest against a maple tree.

My initial reaction was shock. I pulled off to the shoulder of the road a short distance behind the torn-up area where the Toyota left the road, then I fished my cell phone out of my purse and called 911. I remembered the name of the road I was on only because I had just seen a patient whose address was on this same road. After I gave my location to the 911 operator, I approached the car. I could hear a voice coming from inside as I got closer.

"Mom! Mom, are you okay?" The voice sounded young and panicked.

I opened the passenger side door and realized the voice I'd heard belonged to Nick Meyers. He was shaking his mother's shoulder with increasing firmness. He turned to me as I opened his door, and I couldn't tell if he recognized me or if he was just glad someone had shown up to help. "Help us!"

Nick was still strapped into his seat belt, the collapsed airbag in his lap, and a thread of blood trailing down the side of his face. I could see his mother was also strapped in, but she was slumped against the driver's side door and that the side window had shattered in the accident. "Help her! Is she breathing? Help her!" He began to tug at her seat belt to release it.

I heard a hissing sound, and I couldn't tell if the white vapor coming from the front of the car was steam or smoke. In any case, I thought it best to get both of them away from the vehicle. "I'm going to help your mom, but first, I want you to get out of the car and sit over there by that tree." I pointed to a small sapling about forty feet away.

"No, I gotta help my mom!"

"You go over there and wait to flag down the first responders. I'm going to get your mother out now." He let me help him undo his seat belt, and he limped toward the tree I had indicated.

As I ran around to the other side of the car, I could see where the glass from her window dusted the side of Anna's head and shoulder. There were cuts on the side of her face and in her scalp, but they looked superficial. The windshield was broken, and the dashboard looked to be pushed back toward her, but luckily it wasn't pinning her in place. She was breathing, but her respirations were irregular. The vapor I'd seen rising from the engine had turned a dark gray, and I was pretty sure now that it was smoke. I undid Anna's seat belt and started to ease her from the car. I was concerned that she didn't seem to respond when I moved her. I thought maybe she had hit her head so hard on the window or door frame that she was knocked unconscious, but it struck me that Nick had asked right away if she was breathing.

I grabbed Anna under her armpits and dragged her away from the car back toward the grassy patch that bordered the road. I got an initial reaction when I started to drag her but after that, no other response. Nick left his assigned spot by the tree and came to kneel by his mother.

"Is she going to be okay? She's going to be okay, right?" He was crying now.

"Yes, help is on the way." Anna had started to breathe more regularly, but still slower than she should have been. "Nick, what happened? Why did your mother lose control of the car? Was she acting all right before the crash?"

He shook his head, "No."

"Had she been drinking alcohol by any chance?"

He took a big gulping breath, "It's her neck. She takes medication for the pain in her neck. We were on our way home from getting groceries. She said her neck was killing her, she was sweating, and her hands were shaking while we were in Stop and Shop. When we left the store, she took one of her pills. They looked different than the ones she usually has. She was acting normal at first, but then she started looking sleepy and kept shaking her head like she was trying to wake up. I was getting nervous, and I asked her if she was all right, but she wouldn't answer. Then all of a sudden, she, like, passed out, and we were going off the road. You got to give her some of that drug you gave me!"

I heard the approaching emergency vehicles but was still concerned about what had caused Anna to lose consciousness. "Anna, wake up!" There was swelling over her left shoulder area that looked as if she had a fractured left clavicle. I shook her firmly by the right shoulder, and she groaned and tried to open her eyes. I said to Nick, "She is breathing okay now, and I think she is starting to come around." Nick nodded, but he still looked terrified. I saw that as well as having a cut above his right eye, his right hand was reddened and swollen.

While it was still possible that she might have a head injury, what Nick said made it clear she was losing consciousness before the accident. Any number of meds could make her drowsy, but the instructions on the container would warn of this. If she had taken these kinds of meds before, she should have known how the drug affected her. Why would she take something and then drive? He said it was a new drug, though, and that could explain it having a greater effect on her. She was much more sedated when I found her than was typical with the usually prescribed pain medication. Nick had immediately asked if she was breathing and then suggested Narcan. He had had personal experience with having overdosed on an opioid, and a sudden connection occurred to me. Maybe Nick did find the drugs he and the others took that day. Just not where he said, and not from Beck Chandler after all.

There was no time to question Nick then about what I suspected. A small flame was visible, licking around the seams of the Toyota's hood. Anna's eyes had fluttered open briefly, and she had murmured, "What…?" before becoming unconscious again. Nick was standing next to the road now, waving to the emergency vehicles as they approached.

The fire in the car's engine was quickly taken care of by the firefighters before it progressed past the engine compartment. As the paramedics and three police cars arrived, I introduced myself and let them know who Anna and Nick were. One officer took care of blocking off one lane of the road, though I hadn't seen anyone pass since the accident. I saw another officer speaking to Nick; I assumed to get his report of what happened.

I told one of the paramedics what I had observed. "Mrs. Meyers was unresponsive when I removed her from the car. I noticed she had some superficial wounds to her head and face, and I think her left clavicle is broken. According to her son, she took some painkillers for a chronic neck injury several minutes before the accident and seemed to be acting very sleepy and lost consciousness before she lost control of the vehicle and left the road."

As I was speaking, another of the paramedics placed a trauma collar on Anna's neck, and then they both gently loaded her onto a stretcher and into the back of the ambulance. I stood by Nick as they were tending to his mother. Once she was secured in the back of the ambulance, one of the paramedics stayed with Anna to be sure she was stable, and the other came over to examine Nick.

"Hi, buddy. How are you doing? You feel pain anywhere right now?"

Nick raised his right hand in response. He looked pale but seemed to have calmed a bit now that his mother was being taken care of.

The paramedic gently took Nick's hand and said, "Yeah, that looks sore. I think we better take you in to be checked out too. There is another ambulance on the way, and it'll be here in a couple of minutes."

Nick looked panicked now, "Can't I go with my mother?"

"No, you get your own ride, okay? We'll take good care of her, and you can see her later at the hospital."

As the ambulance carrying Anna left, I could hear the approach of the second ambulance. I looked at Nick, and I could see he had tears in his eyes again. "It's okay, like they said, your mom is going to be all right," I said.

A police officer approached us carrying Anna's purse. He went to hand it to Nick. "You want to bring this with you for your mom? It smells a little smokey, but I think the contents are probably still okay."

Nick ignored what the officer was trying to hand him. Instead, he watched as the second ambulance pulled up next to us.

I held out my hand to take the purse.

The police officer looked at me, "You just passing by or do you know these folks."

I looked at Nick, "I'm a... friend. I'll see Mrs. Meyers gets her things."

Nick didn't contradict me, and the officer handed the purse to me.

The second ambulance crew quickly examined Nick and took a set of vital signs. Before they put him in the back of the ambulance, he turned to me and said, "Do you think you could come with me?"

I saw one of the paramedics was about to object, and I said, "How about if I meet you there? I'll wait with you until you get examined, okay?"

He nodded, "Thanks."

I placed Anna's purse on the front seat next to mine. It probably should have gone along with her to the hospital. If she had the medication she took in there, it would be important that the medical staff knew what it was.

I knew that Nick's ambulance would get to the hospital before me, but I needed to make a quick call to my dog walker, Jenny. I needed to let her know I had to tend to an emergency and I would be late getting home, and to ask her if she could feed and stay with Bruno for a while.

When I arrived at the Emergency Department, I was not surprised to find it was extremely busy. I looked for someone I knew from my days as a nurse at University Hospital but did not see anyone I recognized. I approached the front desk and asked to see Nick Meyers.

The receptionist checked her computer. "Are you a relative?"

"No. A family friend. He and his mother were in an accident earlier, and his mother is a patient also. I promised I'd wait with him until he was seen." I wondered again about his father and if he had a relationship with him. I would need to find out if there was any family member we could call since he likely wouldn't need to be admitted, but his mother might.

"We're really busy, as you can see. He's in the hallway outside exam room four." She buzzed me into the back of the unit.

I found Nick lying on a stretcher. He was watching everything going on around him with great interest. His right hand was propped on a pillow. He didn't exactly smile when he saw me, but I thought a look of relief washed over his face.

"Hi. What's going on?" I asked.

"One of the nurses said my mom is stable. I might be able to see her later, they said." He flinched as he tried to raise his right hand slightly. "I'm waiting for them to take an x-ray."

While I was talking to Nick, a woman holding a clipboard came over to us. "Hi. I'm Tyra from the business office. Are you Mom?" She asked me.

"Um, no, I'm just here to give Nick emotional support. His mother was injured in the accident and is also being seen," I said.

She turned to Nick, "Do you have your insurance card on you, hon? Or does your mother have it?"

"It's in my mom's wallet." He nodded to the purse I still had under my arm.

"Oh, I have her purse." I had forgotten to give it to the receptionist at the front desk. I immediately felt guilty. I hoped she was awake enough now to tell them what medication she had taken.

I began to hand it to Nick so he could get his card out of her wallet, but he motioned to his hand and said, "Could you get it out for me?"

When I opened her purse, I saw a jumble of tissues, store receipts, and a baggie of what looked like loose pills. I had expected to find prescription pain relievers in Anna's purse, but I expected to see them in a vial with a label. I hesitated a moment, shaken by the suspicion that another piece of the puzzle had snapped into place.

My thoughts were interrupted by Nick's voice. "I think my mom's card is in there, too, if you need it," he said to Tyra.

I pushed the pills aside and dug out Anna's wallet.

"Look in the compartment near her driver's license. I think that's where she keeps the insurance cards," he told me.

After Tyra got the information she needed, she handed the cards back to me. I placed them back in Anna's wallet, where I found them. As I was putting the wallet back into her purse, I managed to nudge the bag of drugs around a little to get a better look at them. There appeared to be at least fifteen pills in the unmarked bag. I knew what most opioid pain relievers looked like from dealing with some of my patients. These resembled some I'd seen but did not look quite right. There were no manufacturer markings for one thing, and the color was slightly off. I realized Nick was watching me as I had my hand in the purse.

"Okay. We're all set here." Tyra smiled at both of us before she walked away.

Nick had obviously seen me looking at the drugs, so I decided to take a chance and confront him. "Nick, I'm afraid I don't believe you found those drugs you took in the boys' bathroom at school. I think you knew exactly where to get them."

He shook his head, "No. That's not true." He looked away from me for a moment while he said it, and his voice held a certain lack of conviction.

I stared at him levelly, ignoring his comment, then I said, "Did your mom give them to you?" I didn't think that had been the case, but I was waiting to see his reaction.

"Hell no!" He lowered his voice to a harsh whisper. "She had a fit when she found out. She said if I hadn't already almost died, she would kill me for taking them. I had to promise to never take any of her pills again." He gave me a pleading look, "Don't tell that cop friend of yours, okay? I don't want my mom to get in trouble."

"Her doctor must know she is on pain medication. There is nothing wrong with her having those meds if they were prescribed by her physician." I watched for his reaction again.

He looked away from me for several seconds, then started to say, "Look, just please don't…" A nurse walked over to us, followed by an orderly.

"Nick? Let me just check your name band." She checked the band on his wrist and then said, "Sorry it's taking so long for that x-ray, but we had to wait until your mom was awake enough to sign the permit to treat you."

Nick perked up, "She's awake? Can I see her?"

"In a little while. Right now, let Denny here take you to get a picture of that hand."

The orderly turned to me, "I'll have him back in a few minutes."

As Denny wheeled Nick away, the nurse said to me, "I understand you're a friend of Nick's. We called his father. He's on his way." She cleared her throat and said, "His mother told us of their current situation, but I explained to her he needs to be released to a parent or guardian."

I had no real idea of what Anna and her ex's situation was, but I agreed Nick needed to be with a relative. I felt I had to stay with Nick until his father arrived, but I couldn't wait to tell Sunny Cody that Nick had confirmed that he had taken the drugs from his mother. Also, that whatever it was Anna was taking did not look like it came from a pharmacy. That made me think of what Audrey said about Anna seeming to always be around Beck Chandler, and now I believed our suspicions about him dealing drugs were confirmed.

I had a feeling Nick told me all he was going to about where his mother got her drugs, if he even knew. Besides, I thought Anna was the one who needed to supply the rest of the information on what she was on and where she was getting it. Her medical chart would show what pain relievers were originally prescribed for her neck injury, and I knew the staff would question her about what medication she had taken today. I only hoped she would tell them the truth.

True to his promise Denny had Nick back in a few minutes, wheeling him back to his spot by room four. He said someone would be out to let him know what the X-ray showed in a few minutes.

"How did it go?" I asked.

"Okay."

"One of the nurses said that they contacted your father, and he is coming to be with you." He looked a little upset at first. "It's all right; your mom knows."

I could see him relax again, "Okay, cool."

A young man in green scrubs approached us. "Hi, Nick. I'm Dr. Pullum." He went to shake Nick's hand but instead patted his shoulder. "Your x-ray does show a break in two of the bones of your hand. It must have hit the windshield or something in the accident. I'm going to stabilize those bones by putting on a cast so they can heal, okay?"

Once again, Nick was wheeled away. I assumed this time to a treatment room. I felt a bit awkward just standing in the hallway, and I was eager to let Sunny know what was going on, but I didn't want Nick to come back and find no one waiting for him. I didn't have to wait long, though. A man I judged to be in his mid to late forties came rushing toward where I was standing.

"Excuse me. They said I could find my son here."

"Mr. Meyers? They took Nick to put a cast on his hand. He's all right otherwise, though."

I could see a look of relief pass over his face. "That's good." He cleared his throat, "And you are?"

"Melanie Bass. I'm an acquaintance of Nick and Anna's. I was at the scene of the accident, and I told Nick I would stay with him for a while."

"Thank you. That was kind. What happened? They said Anna was stable but that she was going to be admitted?"

"I'm sure the medical staff will update you later, and I think Nick will be eager to fill you in on the accident itself."

We stood in awkward silence for a few minutes. I hated to leave without saying goodbye to Nick, but realized since his father was there now, I really had no reason to stay. I looked at my watch. It was only seven PM. It seemed like we'd been in the ED much longer. I really needed to get home to Bruno, but thought I might press my luck and see if I could get in to see Anna first.

I stopped one of the nurses to ask where Anna was. She checked her computer, then said, "She's undergoing a procedure right now, and then we're waiting for a bed for her on one of the units. You can check back later to see where she was admitted." So, no luck there.

Before I left, I wanted to make sure Anna's purse was returned to her. I wasn't sure what was going to happen as far as the drugs it contained, but I knew I didn't want it in my possession any longer. "I have Mrs. Meyers's purse. It didn't go with her when she was transported here."

"Okay. I'll put it in a personal possessions bag and make sure it's sent with her when she's transported to the floor."

Chapter Thirty-Four

After I got home, I spent a few minutes playing with Bruno, then grabbed a peanut butter and jelly sandwich to calm the rumblings of hunger in my stomach. I decided to go see Sunny Cody in person rather than call her to let her know what I'd found out this afternoon. As I put on my coat to leave, Bruno gave me a mournful look. I couldn't leave him alone again. I snapped on his leash and took him along with me. He had always been good around children, and I knew Sunny's daughter Katie loved dogs.

Shortly after I rang the bell, I could hear the thumping sound of Sunny's cane as she approached to open the door.

She looked from me to Bruno, sitting patiently on his leash by my side. "Well, this is a surprise." She stepped aside to let us in.

"I need to let you know what I found out today, and I wanted to tell you in person. I hope you don't mind I brought Bruno along. He will be a good boy; I promise you," I said.

Just then, there was the sound of running feet coming down the hallway. A pajama-clad Katie appeared. "Oh, you brought your dog! He's so cute!" Katie looked up at me and then her mother, "Is it all right if I pet him?"

Bruno's tail was wagging frantically, "He'd like that," I said. After Katie petted Bruno and got licked several times, I followed Sunny to the living room.

Katie followed along with us, but Sunny said, "Pet the dog one more time, then back to bed young lady." Katie gave Bruno several more pets and ear scratches, but at the sound of her mother clearing her throat, scampered back to her room as she was told.

When Katie was out of earshot, I told Sunny of seeing Anna Meyers going off the road, the injuries she and Nick suffered, and Nick's admission that he took the drugs he gave the other boys from his mother's supply. "Nick said she took some of her 'pain medication' before driving and described her as sleepy and then losing consciousness. I saw some pills in her purse, and they didn't look like they were legally obtained."

"What do you mean?"

"They were loose in a plastic bag and the markings, from what I could see, didn't look like the manufacturer's markings."

"How did you see these pills?" Sunny's voice was a bit sharper than usual.

"An officer at the accident scene gave me her purse to bring to her. At the hospital, Nick asked me to take out their insurance cards, and while I was doing that, I saw the pills."

"So, you had permission to look in her purse?"

"Well, from her son, yes. Plus, I needed to get information needed by the hospital treating them." I hoped my explanation would prove I had reason to search Anna's purse.

"Okay, where is Anna's purse now?"

"I turned it over to one of the nurses. She put it in a personal effects bag with Anna's name on it."

"You said her nurse told you she had regained consciousness?" Sunny looked at her watch, "Let me see if anyone from law enforcement has had a chance to question her yet."

While Sunny made her call, I sat and petted Bruno, trying to get a grip on the jumble of emotions I was feeling. I felt a jolt of excitement that I may have found a link to solving one of the cases Sunny was involved in. But I also felt sorry for Anna that she had gotten caught up in a web of addiction to painkillers and what that might mean to her family.

When Sunny ended her call, she said, "I spoke with an Officer Rogers from the New Haven Police Department. He was very accommodating once I identified myself and told him what my interest was in the case. He said they were sending an officer now to talk to Anna Meyers, and he would let me know what they found out. He said the hospital sent a toxicology screen on her, but the results are still pending. She told the staff what she was on, but it looks like this batch, at least, was obviously cut with something."

"If Beck Chandler was supplying her with her drugs, I wonder if he sold her these before he left or if she got them from someone else," I said.

"That's one of the things the officer will find out. I mentioned to Rogers that we were looking for Beck Chandler to question him, but that he had dropped out of sight. He said if he got any information on Chandler's whereabouts, he'd give me a call."

I had another thought. "What about Detective Langley? Shouldn't he be notified of what we discovered about where the pills came from?" I knew Sunny had very little use for him, but he was the one who was supposed to be primarily investigating the case. Plus, maybe it would defuse his anger at me getting involved in the investigation if he knew I had gotten some useful information.

I thought Sunny would be upset with me for mentioning that Langley should be informed, but instead, she just leaned back in her chair and said, "Yes. I'll let him know. But first, I want to see what New Haven finds out."

Not for the first time, I had a feeling that it wasn't strictly protocol the way Sunny was handling the investigation. I did trust her to get results, however.

Bruno had fallen asleep at my feet, and I realized it was getting late. "I may as well go home. The toxicology results will be back soon, but it may be a while before you hear back from Officer Rogers. You will let me know what you find out though?"

Sunny stretched and yawned, "Yes, I'll call you tomorrow and let you know what I can."

I took that as a reminder that while I was free to share what information I gathered, Sunny was still bound to keep confidential some aspects of the case.

Sunny called me, as promised, the next day at lunchtime to say that Anna Meyers's tox screen had come back positive for opioids. This was what we expected. They had run a routine screen for the usual abused drugs, which would not pick up any additives to the pills but they were testing for whatever the pills had been cut with now.

"Also, no surprise, Anna admitted that she had been getting her pills from Chandler. When he was no longer around, she got her last batch from a guy she found hanging around outside the methadone clinic in New Haven. She didn't know his name but gave his description to the officer who interviewed her." Sunny hesitated a moment, then continued, "I did call Langley to let him know about Anna Meyers."

"What did he say?" I had a feeling he wasn't pleased at not being notified at once.

"He used a good deal of language I won't repeat, but he wanted to know where Chandler was and accused me of holding out on him so I could make the arrest myself. He threatened to have me written up and to have you arrested for interfering in a police investigation."

My stomach dropped at that last bit of news.

"Don't worry; he won't do either of those things. I heard his investigative skills haven't exactly impressed the higher ups, and this will only accentuate the lack of progress he is making. I called the Chief first thing this morning to keep him up to date on what was going on with the case. I told him you were a citizen who came upon information that was useful to us."

"Thanks."

"I also wanted to let you know that I've been cleared to return to light duty. I'm going back tomorrow."

"That's great!" I had another thought, though. "How did Katie react when you told her?"

"She was a little upset at first. But I resorted to the time-honored bribe of promising her a special surprise. Besides, my mother and father, bless them, watch her while I'm at work. They spoil her rotten, so that will take the sting out of me not being home all the time."

"Thank you for letting me know what Anna said and for defending me to your chief. If I happen to pick up any more information that might help with your investigation, I'll be sure to contact you."

After I ended my call from Sunny, I felt a sense of regret mixed with relief that I probably wouldn't need to do any more of Sunny's leg work. However, I still had several more patients to see that day, so I didn't have much time to dwell on what she had told me or the fact that there were still aspects of the case that hadn't been solved.

Chapter Thirty-Five

I was excited about my dinner date with Justin on Wednesday evening. We had reservations at Café Fiore, my favorite Italian restaurant, and after the intense start to my week, I was looking forward to a relaxing evening reconnecting with each other. When I saw his name come up on the display on my cell phone at five PM, however, I got a bad feeling.

"Hi, Melanie." Right away, there was something in the tone of his voice that tipped me off to the fact this would not be good news. "I'm so sorry, but I'll have to cancel dinner tonight. Dr. Reddy has come down with the flu, so I need to take call for the practice. I've got two emergencies coming in, and I don't know when I'll be done dealing with them."

I felt disappointed, but I certainly couldn't argue that under the circumstances, he had no choice but to cancel our plans. "Oh, that's too bad, I was really looking forward to tonight. I understand though."

"How about we try again on Friday? Maybe Martin will be feeling better by then, or I can get a vet from another practice to take my calls for the evening."

"Friday sounds good. I hope your emergencies go well. I want to update your grandfather on something anyway. I want to tell him how part of that case I was working on with Detective Cody turned out. I'll take a ride over to his place tonight and see how he is doing. I might also tease him a little about how his meddling helped get us back together," I said.

"Okay. If I'm done here early enough, I'll stop over there too. We can go for a cup of coffee or something afterward."

"I'd like that." When I got off the phone I sighed and said to Bruno, "I guess there is no Shrimp Scampi for me tonight." I could swear he gave me a sympathetic look.

Charlie looked surprised when he opened the door and found me on his doorstep.

"I thought you and Justin had a date for tonight!"

I squinted my eyes at him. "Just how much about our relationship is Justin sharing with you? We did have plans, but he had to deal with a couple of last-minute emergencies at work. I wanted to come and see you anyway. He said he'll stop over here later."

After we were settled in the living room I said, "Have you been taking your blood pressure and reporting it back to your doctor like we discussed?"

"Yes. I'm passing with flying colors, according to the doc."

"Good. Another reason I wanted to see you was I wanted to let you know that we found out where Nick Meyers got the drugs he and the other boys used." I told him about the accident and finding the pills in Anna Meyers' possession.

"Apparently, Anna took a bad fall a little over a year and a half ago and suffered an injury to her neck. She admitted to getting addicted to her pain medication. Eventually, however, her primary physician refused to write her any more prescriptions and told her she should be all right with over-the-counter medication. She said she was complaining of how much pain she was in at a soccer game shortly after that. She mentioned she couldn't get the meds that worked for her. Chandler overheard her and pulled her aside after the game and said he might be able to help her out."

Charlie shook his head, "Some help."

"When Beck Chandler disappeared, she had to look for a new dealer. The pill she took the day of the accident was the first one from that batch, and it contained some other substance."

"She going to be all right?" Charlie asked.

"As far as the accident, I'd say so. She suffered a few broken bones and cuts, but no life-threatening injuries. As far as her drug problem, I'm afraid she's going to need treatment."

"I feel sorry for the boy," Charlie said. "He say what made him decide to take some of her pills the day you found them at the soccer field?"

"Nick swears it was the first time he did that. He said the guys were feeling under a lot of pressure to win the championship for the school, and he thought the drugs would relax them a little."

"So, what will happen to the kid now?"

"Anna agreed he could stay with his father while she got her addiction under control. She also needs to see what's going to happen as far as any charges against her."

Our conversation was interrupted by the sound of Charlie's phone.

I watched him as he listened to whoever was on the other end. He was nodding at whatever the person was telling him, but then suddenly, his eyebrows shot up. "You sure? Okay. Well, thanks, Stu. Yeah, we'll get together soon."

After he ended the call, he said, "I'll be damned! That was my friend Stu, the guy who owns the body shop. He said he went through the records from the past few weeks for repairs done while he was away. He found a bill for the repair of right front-end damage on a 2015 gray Camry. He talked to his son-in-law and the son-in-law said he remembers the old lady who brought it in because she seemed so upset. She said she misjudged the distance pulling into her garage and hit the frame of the garage door. She wanted to pay for the damage herself rather than going through insurance. She said she didn't want her family to know about it. She told him her kids would take her car away, saying she was too old to drive anymore. The car belongs to Emma Reynolds."

"You're kidding."

He shook his head, "No. I suppose she could have hit the frame of the garage door. But I don't remember hearing any loud bangs or anything."

I stood up and went for my jacket, where it hung by the door. "I can't see that this has anything to do with what happened with Detective Cody, but I don't think it will hurt to just go to talk with her and find out exactly what happened."

Charlie hoisted himself up out of his chair and said, "I'll come too. You probably shouldn't go alone."

I laughed, "Even if what she told your friend doesn't check out, don't you think I can handle an eighty-two-year-old woman on my own? I know Mrs. Reynolds can be feisty, but I don't think there is any reason to worry."

He sat back down, his disappointment evident by the look on his face. "I wasn't saying you can't handle her; I'm just interested to hear her explanation firsthand."

"Keep your phone next to you. If I need backup, I'll call you." I hid my smile as I closed the door behind me.

I decided to walk the short distance next door to Mrs. Reynolds's house. As I was going up her driveway, I saw headlights turn into Charlie's driveway. Justin must have finished with his emergencies and come to meet me at his grandfather's as he promised.

Before going up to Emma Reynolds's front door, I walked over to look at her garage. I took out my phone to use the light to examine both sides of each bay to the two-car garage. There was no damage that I could see anywhere on either frame, nor did it look like there had been any recent repairs made. In fact, I noticed a large spider web in the corner where one of the doors met the frame. Her explanation to the body shop did not check out, but I suppose there could be an even more embarrassing explanation for the damage to her car that she didn't want to give.

Once again it took a few minutes before Mrs. Reynolds answered the door. I chalked up the delay to the fact that in spite of the fact Charlie said she was unusually spry for her age, she had been ill recently. She might be moving more slowly as she recovered.

The door finally opened a crack. "Oh, I wasn't expecting anyone. This is late for you to be making a call, isn't it?" She opened the door wider but stood firmly blocking my way in.

"I'm not here..."

"I'm just fine now, and this is not a good time, I'm afraid." She gave me a strained smile.

"I won't keep you long. May I come in? I just wanted to ask you about something."

"What is it I can help you with?" She didn't move from her position in the doorway.

"I really think it would be better if we stepped inside to talk." It was obvious she didn't want to let me into the house. I couldn't imagine why, but I was beginning to get a strange feeling.

She hesitated but then said loudly, "All right, come on in then."

Just as I was stepping inside, I heard a loud bang coming from down the hallway toward what I assumed were the bedrooms.

"That dang cat. I can't imagine what she's gotten into now!" I thought Mrs. Reynolds sounded more nervous than upset.

She led me into the living room and motioned to a chair, "You may as well have a seat, but as I said, this isn't a good time for you to visit."

As Emma sat opposite me on the sofa, I saw her cat, Pancake, dart out from behind it and take off for the kitchen. She had been nowhere near whatever was down the hallway. Emma sat stiffly on the sofa, an expectant look on her face.

"I came because I need to ask you about some damage to your car that happened a couple of weeks ago."

I saw a look of surprise quickly pass over her face. "I don't know what you're...oh that! I had a little accident pulling into my garage. So silly. How did you happen to hear about it?"

I ignored her question. "I'm curious how that could be. I didn't see any damage to your garage."

"Well, of course, I had it repaired. The door wouldn't have closed properly if I hadn't. The car is fixed now too." Her voice was calm, but I noticed she kept fastening and unfastening the Velcro holding the splint on her left wrist.

"You have a 2015 Toyota Camry, don't you?"

"I don't know what business that is of yours or why you are asking me these questions. You better go now." She got up from her perch on the sofa.

I stayed seated and said, "I was a witness to an incident a few weeks ago where a police officer was injured and another man shot. One of the cars involved matches the description of your vehicle. I was wondering if I could look at your car."

"No! That's ridiculous!" She sat down again.

"If you don't want to let me look at the car to see if I recognize it, I'm afraid I'm going to have to call the police. They..."

"No! Don't call the police! I'll..."

She was interrupted by a loud hacking cough coming from down the hallway. Both Mrs. Reynolds and I sat frozen in place. Mrs. Reynolds spoke first, "That's my grandson. He's staying with me. He's not feeling well." As if on cue, I heard another bout of coughing, though this time, it sounded like he was trying to smother the sound.

I remembered Charlie mentioning Mrs. Reynolds having a grandson who came to visit her periodically. Charlie didn't think too much of him, but no matter how irresponsible or loud Charlie thought he was, he didn't sound like he was in good shape right now. "He sounds like he has a serious respiratory infection. It's possible he became infected with whatever you had." I stood up. "I could examine him if you like. He might need to be seen by his..."

A hoarse voice coming from the doorway interrupted me. "Sit down. I'll be fine."

I turned to see Beck Chandler standing there, pointing a gun at me. He looked ghastly.

He was pale, he had an audible wheeze, and the hand holding the gun was shaking slightly.

Mrs. Reynolds was looking at him in horror. "Beck, where did you get that gun?"

He continued to point the wavering gun at me, "It's going to be okay, Grandma. Just get me some more of that medicine from on top of the refrigerator, please."

Mrs. Reynolds gave me a wide-eyed look, then got up to do as he asked. I sat stock still in my chair, trying to hide my shock at realizing that Beck Chandler was Mrs. Reynolds's grandson. His disappearance and then the fact that she was reluctant to go to the hospital or even let me in to see her when she was sick a week ago now made sense. "Beck, I don't know if you remember me, but I came to the soccer field to talk to you a while ago. May I get my ID badge from my purse?" I bent to fiddle around in my purse as if looking for my ID but intending to grab my phone.

"Get your hand out of your purse." He waved the gun at me.

I did as he said, slowly withdrawing my hand.

"I remember you. You thought I gave the boys the pills they took." His grandmother came back with a bottle of cold and flu medication and poured a dose for him. He began to cough deeply again as he swallowed it, but he was able to keep the gun steady enough that I didn't want to take a chance on any sudden moves. Mrs. Reynolds didn't seem to know what to do next, so she went to sit on the sofa where she had been.

"That's true, but now I know what really happened. Nick admitted he took the pills from his mother. Anna was in an accident two days ago, and it became obvious she was using illegal drugs. She's already told the police that you were the one selling them to her."

"She's okay, though?" He had gone to stand with one hand on the back of one of the chairs opposite me. He appeared to be leaning on it.

"She's going to be all right, but you really don't look well. You need to get more treatment than over-the-counter medicine for that respiratory infection. The police are looking for you, and I don't think you'll get too far in your condition. It would be better if you just turned yourself in." He coughed again, not as loudly, but he was flushed now like he had a fever.

He looked unsteady as he shuffled to sit in the chair he had been leaning on. "I can't turn myself in." He was still holding the gun, but it was angled more toward the floor now. "You said you were there that day on Windy Reed Road? You saw what happened to Bourne. I'll be dead before I make bail if I get arrested."

I felt a block of ice wedge itself in my stomach. I thought of the Camry. "You were driving your grandmother's car!" I glanced at Mrs. Reynolds, who looked as if she wanted to sink into the floor.

"Langley said to be sure to get a less conspicuous car than my Mustang."

"Langley? Detective Langley?"

He nodded, "He said I only had to drive some guy who was making a drop-off. But then this guy shoots Bourne and then grabs the wheel and pulls us toward the lady cop. Next thing I know, he's got the gun pointed at my head and says if I stop or say anything to anyone about what just happened, I'm next."

"Why did Detective Langley want you involved in what happened that day on Windy Reed?"

The gun was resting on his knee now. I realized I might be able to make a dash for the door then, but I sat glued to my seat, waiting for him to answer. "He said I owe him for taking care of that issue with the pills they found in my possession last spring. He made the pills, and the charge against me, disappear. I wish I'd let them arrest me then."

I felt a little sick to my stomach now. "Langley is involved in this whole thing?"

"Completely." The medication he took must have helped a little because he still looked terrible but wasn't coughing as much. "You can't call the cops because Langley will see to it something 'accidentally' happens to me. He blamed me when those kids overdosed. He didn't believe me when I said I hadn't sold them the pills. He said I was getting sloppy. That all the parents were up in arms, and there was going to be a big stink until they found out who did it. He said I better not give anybody any information that could connect him to the operation, either. He saw me talking to you that day and threatened me. He told me he'd say he discovered I was driving the car that day, and he'd arrest me for attempted murder and assault on an officer. If something happened to me after I was arrested, who's to say it wasn't retaliation from Bourne's associates? I nearly killed a cop, so if I was dead, there probably wouldn't be too many tears shed."

Even though I knew Cody said she thought Langley was bad at his job, I was sickened to hear that he was actually a bad cop. "What made you decide to disappear?"

"He came to my apartment a few days ago. He said the pressure was increasing to bring me in on suspicion of possession of narcotics with intent to sell. Langley said it might be better for all of us if I 'relocated.' He said he could help me with that. I've seen how he helped 'relocate' people he didn't want to talk, so I took off. I only meant to stay here a day or two until I figured something else out. Then my grandmother got sick. I couldn't leave her alone like that."

I remembered Chandler's roommate mentioning the rough-looking guy who came looking for him after the visit from Langley and realized he was right about being in danger.

Chandler raised the gun again and pointed it at me, "I need to leave now."

He still looked shaky, and I didn't think he would get far. After what he told me, I was afraid to take a chance with the police being called until it was clear what was going on. I needed to keep him here until I could get word to Sunny about what he told me.

"My friends know I came to talk to your grandmother. It's been a long time now, and they're going to call the police. I believe what you told me. Let me text them and tell them I'm all right." He didn't respond, but kept the gun pointed at me as I slowly reached for my phone in my purse. I texted: *all okay do not call police* and held it up so Chandler could see.

Then I said, "I know one of the detectives investigating what happened the day Bourne was shot. She'll listen to you. She doesn't trust Langley either. Let me text her, too." I didn't mention she was the one he hit.

He hesitated a moment as if thinking about it, "No. Bring me your phone now." He held out his hand.

But before I handed it to him, I quickly added *call cody* and hit send. He grabbed the phone and, without looking at it again, placed it face down on the side table near him. I heard the ding of a response to my text, but Chandler never picked up the phone to check what it said.

He looked as if he wasn't sure how to keep an eye on me and, at the same time, prepare to leave. I was resigned to the fact that he was going to come to the obvious conclusion he needed to tie me up when he said, "Grandma, could you get my things from my room and put them in my duffle?" He was hoarse, and his words were interrupted by fits of coughing again. "Also, pack some water and the medicine."

Emma got up, but then paused and said, "Maybe you should let her call her friend. What if you get stopped..."

Beck shook his head. "No."

She gave me a worried look as she went to get the things he requested. As she headed out of the room, he called after her, "Bring some rope or twine, too."

He had been aiming the gun at me, but now was letting the barrel drift down toward the floor again as if the gun was getting too heavy. I considered again just running for the door in hopes that his reaction time was slowed.

There was a soft thump at the front door. Chandler jerked his head in that direction, raising his gun as he did so. Suddenly the door burst open, and a voice said, "Put the gun down." Detective Langley had his gun pointed at Chandler. When he noticed me, he said, "Just don't take a hint, do you?" He grabbed me by the arm, pulling me up out of the chair and twisting my left arm up behind me. I could feel the pressure as he held his gun against my head behind my ear. I was aware of a nauseating metallic smell. "I said drop your weapon Chandler."

Beck hesitated a moment, continuing to point his gun at Langley, but then threw it on the floor. Langley said, "Now kick it over here and put your hands on the arms of the chair."

My thoughts were racing. I had no idea how Langley found Chandler, but I deeply regretted telling Charlie not to call the police.

I fought to keep my voice calm as I said, "Detective Langley..."

The pressure on my arm increased, "Quiet! Pick up his gun and hand it to me."

He let go of my arm, and I felt the pressure of the gun shift to my back as I bent to do as he said.

After I handed him the gun, he looked at it, then he swore under his breath, and tossed it across the room. "You are a screw-up! It's not even loaded." He hesitated a moment as if he was thinking, then said, "This is how it will play out: Miss Bass found you and threatened to call the police, and you shot her. I came in and had to take you down and..." He stopped, "where's the old lady that lives here?"

I felt the whoosh of air caused by swift movement. "Here!" There was the sound of something heavy hitting bone twice in rapid succession. Detective Langley crumpled against me, nearly causing me to fall forward. I turned to see Emma Reynolds standing there with a metal meat tenderizing mallet in her good hand and a satisfied look on her face.

Langley lay sprawled on the floor, not moving. Chandler leapt up and kicked his gun away from him.

I quickly checked Langley for a pulse, concerned Emma had stopped him permanently, but then I saw him make a small movement with his right hand.

"Hurry before he regains consciousness! We need to call the police now." Chandler didn't respond but didn't stop me when I reached to grab my phone from the table.

I had just started to make the call when someone shouted "Police!" and the door burst open again. "Hands on your heads!"

Emma dropped her mallet on the floor, and we all did as instructed. One of the officers bent to check on Langley, then I heard him call for an ambulance. Another officer said, "You can put your hands down, but remain exactly where you are."

I said, "Officers, Detective Langley was threatening us and..."

"I hit him. He was going to shoot Miss Bass." Emma said. She sounded much calmer than I felt.

The officer who appeared to be in charge said, "All right, I'm going to need all of you to come down to the station. Once we're there, we can sort out what exactly happened here."

I heard a tapping noise coming from the entranceway, and Detective Cody came into the room, followed by Officer Bridges. She showed her ID and said, "I'd like to be there when you interview them if you don't mind." I swore I saw her give Langley's side a short kick as she passed him.

I was escorted out by one of the officers. He explained that I wasn't being arrested...yet. That I was just being asked to come in and give my version of what happened.

As I put my phone back into my purse, I saw the text Charlie had sent. In reply to mine telling him not to call the police, Charlie had texted back *too late, Justin did already.* Bless Justin, and bless him for calling Cody too.

As we were led out, I could see that there were multiple police cars waiting outside, and the ambulance for Langley was just pulling up. There was also a throng of neighbors gathered, trying to see what happened. I searched the crowd to see Charlie and Justin being held back by a female officer.

They both looked relieved to see I was all right, but nothing could match the relief I felt. I asked the officer escorting me if I could speak with them quickly. I leaned in and gave Charlie a peck on the cheek, "Thank you." My kiss for Justin was less chaste. As I pulled away, he said, "We *really* need to stop meeting like this!"

Chapter Thirty-Six

We were taken to the police station in separate cars. I didn't see Mrs. Reynolds again as I was led to an interview room, but I caught a glimpse of Beck Chandler in handcuffs as he was being led to another part of the station.

I gave my statement to one of the officers, but when I got to the part about Langley bursting in and holding me at gunpoint, it was hard to keep my voice from wavering. Once I was done, he asked me to wait until he was sure they were through questioning me and left the room. As soon as he had gone, Sunny Cody came in to speak to me.

"I don't know how Langley figured out where Chandler was. I had no idea he was at Mrs. Reynolds or that he was her grandson," I said.

"Your friend Dr. McKenzie called the station and asked to speak to me. He said it was concerning the vehicle we were looking for in relation to the shooting and my hit-and-run. However, I was in a meeting with the chief. The dispatcher knew Langley had been on the case and connected Dr. McKenzie to him instead. I guess Langley figured he might find Chandler there since that was where he borrowed the car. Luckily, the dispatcher also told me about the call as soon as I was out of the meeting. Part of the meeting had to do with new information about Langley. I notified the Guilford police telling them the situation."

"Where is Langley now?"

Sunny made a disgusted sound, "At the emergency department being checked out. He has already been taken into custody, though, pending a thorough investigation of his actions. Chandler isn't the only one who claims

Langley was involved in the narcotics ring. That was why I was meeting with the Chief. Reno Kemp was arrested in Torrington on a grand larceny charge. He says he would like to make a deal for a reduced charge. He's willing to testify that Langley set up the deal on Windy Reed Road and that he ordered the hit on Bourne." She took a deep breath as if to calm herself. "They are reopening Brian's case also. Kemp says he was with Tackman the night Brian was killed and will confirm Langley's report was falsified. That's all I can say for now."

Suddenly I flashed back to the feel of Langley's gun when he had it pressed against my head, and I shivered. "So, Langley wasn't so much lazy as trying to make sure no one was arrested who could connect him to the narcotics operation."

"Yes, it certainly looks that way."

Officer Bridges popped his head into the room, "Sunny, can you come here a minute?"

Shortly after Sunny left the room, another officer came in to tell me I was free to leave. They said that they would contact me with any further questions. I was mentally and physically exhausted by this time. Suddenly, it occurred to me that I would need a ride home. I took out my phone to call Justin, but when I walked out of the station, I saw he was parked in front, waiting for me. He immediately jumped out of the car and rushed to embrace me.

"You weren't hurt, were you? I should have gone right over to Mrs. Reynolds when my grandfather told me why you were going to talk to her!"

I pulled away to look at him. Justin appeared as wrung out as I felt, "No. I think it's a good thing you didn't come over. I'm not sure how things would have gone if you showed up when I discovered Chandler was there."

"I overheard the police talking; they said he held you at gunpoint."

I thought of how Chandler had let the gun drift at times and what Langley had said, "Yes, but the gun wasn't loaded. Though I certainly didn't know that at the time." I was beginning to shake with fatigue. "Could we leave now? I'll explain everything once we're in the car."

CHAPTER THIRTY-SIX

Once I told Justin everything that had happened at Mrs. Reynolds, he was quiet for a moment. Then he said, "I can't help but feel like I am partly at fault for putting you in danger this time. It sounds like Chandler was about to escape without hurting you. It was my fault Langley showed up."

"But you didn't know Langley wasn't to be trusted. I didn't realize he was involved in the narcotics ring until Chandler told me."

"Even so. I'm sorry."

"Next time I get involved in something like this, I'll just have to make sure I keep you firmly in the loop."

I was joking, but Justin turned to me and said, "Yes, please. Maybe if I'm involved, I can keep an eye on you and won't worry so much."

I was so tired I just wanted to go home. Bruno had been alone for a long time, and I was sure was wondering what had happened to me. I told Justin I would get a ride to pick up my car at his grandfather's in the morning.

When we got to my house, Justin walked me to my door. "I hope you won't mind if I don't invite you in," I said. "All I want right now is to get some sleep."

"Of course. But I'll come over tomorrow." He checked his watch. "Make that later today." He bent to kiss me good night.

Despite all the events of the evening, I slept soundly until my alarm woke me. Once I was awake, however, my mind raced with thoughts about all that had happened in the past weeks. I was thankful I had the day off. After I fed Bruno and had my own breakfast, I decided to take Bruno on a long walk to clear my head.

When we got back, I called Lynn hoping that she was free to drive me to Charlie Duggan's house to pick up my car. I also knew she would want me to fill her in on what had happened the previous night.

"Sure, I'll be by in fifteen minutes if that works for you. I'm teaching a class at the Senior Center later today, but I have time now." Lynn said.

On the way to Charlie's house, I told her about finding Chandler, what happened with Langley, and his plan to make it look like Chandler shot me, and then he shot Chandler while capturing him. That part was difficult to tell. I chuckled, though, when I related how Mrs. Reynolds had taken out

Langley with a kitchen implement.

Lynn swerved a little when I told her about Langley holding a gun to my head. I realized I probably should have saved that part for when we weren't moving.

"I assume both Langley and Chandler are under arrest, but will Mrs. Reynolds be charged with anything?" Lynn asked.

"I don't know. She was defending us against Langley when she hit him, but she also was harboring a criminal. I'll have to ask Sunny Cody when I talk to her next."

We were almost at Charlie's when I realized she hadn't told me what happened when Alex approached his mother about hiring Ames to investigate her. "Did you get an apology from Mrs. Drover?"

Lynn shrugged, "In a way, yes. I got a lovely bouquet of fall flowers with a note that said 'Please forgive me' signed D.D."

"That's good, right? I mean, a phone call would have been better, but she did send flowers," I said. I thought Mrs. Drover could have been more personal in her note, but at least it looked like she made an effort.

Lynn sighed, "I don't want to sound ungrateful, but the flowers came from the shop Alex always uses, and he seemed to know what kind of bouquet his mother sent before I mentioned it."

"Oh." I didn't know what else to say to that.

"I have been thinking a lot about what you said about Alex and me only having dated a few months. I love him, but I've been thinking maybe we shouldn't rush into our marriage just yet. A summer wedding would be beautiful, and I could use the extra time while we are planning it to get to know his family a bit better."

I tried to hide my relief, "That sounds like a plan. I love summer weddings."

Charlie came out onto his front stoop as soon as Lynn pulled away.

"Come on in. I been waiting all morning to hear the full story."

Charlie put the water on for tea before we settled in his living room. After I took him through everything that happened at Mrs. Reynolds's, Charlie said, "I told you Emma was a lively one. I only wish I was there to help."

"You were the one to provide the key to finding Chandler when you talked to your friend Stu."

"Yeah, true." He seemed satisfied by that fact. "Wouldn't have minded being in on the action, though." He cocked an eyebrow at me, "Maybe next time."

I started to object, but then realized he was just kidding. I hoped.

A week and a half later, I got a text from Sunny Cody asking me to stop over at her house.

When she opened the door, I could see that Sunny was definitely more stable on her injured leg, though she still was using her cane.

"Come in." We went to our usual spot in her living room." I have something I need to show you, but first, let me say thank you for all the help you gave me in my investigation."

"I hope you didn't get in trouble over my being involved." Despite being a creep, I knew Langley was probably right that I had no business being involved in a police investigation.

Sunny said, "Mmph. Not too much trouble. I can deal with it."

There was the sound of running, and Katie burst into the room, followed by an adorable chocolate lab puppy. "See, Miss Bass! Mommy got me a puppy! I named her Beanie."

Sunny smiled, "That is what I wanted to show you. I should say, Katie wanted to show you." She went to the coffee table where, from underneath her usual jumble of papers, she pulled a book titled *The Puppy Care Bible*. "I'm doing my homework since you once accused me of knowing nothing about dogs. However, I'll be counting on your assistance once again, I'm afraid."

I bent to rub Beanie's belly as she rolled over in front of me. "I'd love to help you. It so happens I know a wonderful veterinarian, too!"

Acknowledgements

I would like to thank Roberta Isleib (AKA Lucy Burdette) and Ang Pompano for the advice, support, and encouragement they have provided me over the more than twenty years we have been together as a writers group. In tough times and in good we have resolved to continue to "Press on brave souls."

I owe thanks to Annette Pompano, Joann Pompano, and Rochelle Hastings for sharing their experiences with orthopedic surgery and its aftermath.

I was thrilled to be able to attend the Guilford Police Department's Citizen's Police Academy this spring. It gave me great insight into how the police department works, and a tremendous respect for these wonderful police officers. Unfortunately, this made it difficult to pretend that any police department in the area could be less than stellar. All mistakes and liberties taken with police procedure and integrity are mine.

I want to thank Rich, Josh, Laura, and Jeffrey for their constant encouragement, help, and love. And a shout out to my dog, Toby, for accompanying me on our daily walks on the trail that inspired Windy Reed Road.

About the Author

Christine Falcone is recently retired after nearly forty years as an RN in a Neonatal Intensive Care Unit. Her short stories have appeared in publications such as *Imagine, Lancrom Review,* and *Deadfall*: Crime Stories by New England writers. *Ex'd Out,* the first in her Melanie Bass Mystery Series, was published in 2022. She is a member of Sisters in Crime and Mystery Writers of America.

She lives on the Connecticut Shoreline with her family and a dog who is not nearly as well behaved as Bruno, the beloved canine in her novel.

SOCIAL MEDIA HANDLES:
Christine Falcone Author – (FB)
@christi77865450 (twitter)

AUTHOR WEBSITE:
christinefalcone.com

Also by Christine Falcone

Ex'd Out – book one in the Melanie Bass Mystery Series

Printed in the USA
CPSIA information can be obtained
at www.ICGtesting.com
LVHW041334171123
764112LV00064B/1950